Leslie Paine is one of that great band of brothers and sisters whose common ground is a rugby pitch. He has pursued the oval ball on fields throughout the country, both as player (Bath, Rosslyn Park, Cambridge City), and reporter (The Times, Cambridge Evening News). He's spoken at more rugby club suppers than he's had hot dinners and has a collection of rare rugby books than any front row forward would envy.

He is the author of that apparent oxymoron 'The Wit of Rugby' and a contributor to that other sporting classic, 'A Funny Thing Happened On The Way to Twickenham'.

UNCLE R REMEMBERS...
THE FUNNY SIDE OF RUGBY

Leslie Paine

UNCLE R REMEMBERS... THE FUNNY SIDE OF RUGBY

Vanguard Press

VANGUARD PAPERBACK

© Copyright 2004
Leslie Paine

The right of Leslie Paine to be identified as author of
this work has been asserted by him in accordance with the
Copyright, Designs and Patents Act 1988

All Rights Reserved

No reproduction, copy or transmission of this publication
may be made without written permission.
No paragraph of this publication may be reproduced,
copied or transmitted save with the written permission of the
publisher, or in accordance with the provisions
of the Copyright Act 1956 (as amended).

Any person who does any unauthorised act in relation to
this publication may be liable to criminal
prosecution and civil claims for damage.

A CIP catalogue record for this title is
available from the British Library
ISBN 1 843860 79 1

*Vanguard Press is an imprint of
Pegasus Elliot MacKenzie Publishers Ltd.*
www.pegasuspublishers.com

Illustrations by Sally Brodholt

First Published in 2004

**Vanguard Press
Sheraton House Castle Park
Cambridge England**

Printed & Bound in Great Britain

Dedication

To the City of Bath (now Beechen Cliff) School where I first picked up the ball and ran with it; Cambridge City Rugby Club which provided me with a host of friends and some of the happiest years of my rugby life; and to my sternest critic: my wife Sally – who bravely bore the burden of listening to me ad nauseam during the gestation period of this book.

Chapter 1

Uncle R Remembers

Some old men forget. Some don't. My Uncle Ronnie – Uncle R to the family for as long as I can remember – is one who doesn't.

Particularly anything to do with rugby, and especially Mellstock rugby.

An oval ball addict since childhood, he's also a genuine rugby romantic. Head full of male bonding, old heroes and ancient matches, he's the only man I know who can hear Twickenham described as a 'Temple of the Sacred Egg' and not burst out laughing.

And as for Mellstock RUFC, he worships it with

the sort of all-consuming passion that other men reserve for motor cars, soccer and sex.

In the wider world of the handling code he's been hit hard these past few years by the coming of professionalism. And even now mention of players strutting their stuff for six figure salaries, and millionaire businessmen buying up rugby clubs lock, stock and every last beer barrel can set the blood thundering in his ears and the veins in his temples bulging.

But to good old highly unprofessional Mellstock whose cause he's served, man and boy these fifty years, his dedication remains steadfast and undiminished.

These days of course, time has at last started to catch up with him. Uncle R, already retired, teeters on the brink of the sere and yellow leaf. But if you think that just because they've given him his bus pass, he's ready to don slippers and cardigan and start singing 'Old Rockin' Chair's Got Me', you've got another think coming.

On the other hand, getting the old freedom pass, like being told you're to be hanged in the morning, does tend to concentrate the mind a bit and remind you that Time's Winged Chariot could be closer than you think. Which is why, when Uncle R got his, he decided that the time had come to review his lifestyle in the light of his new-found status.

It didn't take him long. For a man who's never been known to refuse a drink in his life, the decision wasn't exactly difficult. He became the self-appointed, official custodian of the Mellstock RFC's bar: an appointment hastily and gratefully confirmed by the club. And ever since has devoted his days to making its beer the best in town. Tapping, testing, tasting, he pursues the perfect pint like Sir Galahad after the Holy Grail, and he enjoys every minute of it.

A typical Victorian sports pavilion well past its sell-by date.

But what he enjoys even more is having the right to be in the Mellstock pavilion whenever and for however long he chooses.

He loves the place.

And if you wonder why, why a grown man should be so absorbed in an old-fashioned, run-down, green-painted, red-roofed, veranda-fronted, typical wooden Victorian sports pavilion well past its sell-by date – the answer's simple.

He's spent half his life there. For fifty years or more it's been the centre of his leisure existence. He's changed, bathed, dined and got drunk in it; sung his songs, told his jokes, reminisced and bored in it; danced, flirted and canoodled in it; shouted, bawled, argued and pontificated in it, and spent a thousand and one boozy nights in it carousing with his teammates and afternoon opponents.

No wonder then that that musty, stud-pocked old edifice, redolent of wintergreen, stale tobacco, cheese and pickle sandwiches, meat pie suppers, and a century of mud, sweat and beers, means a lot to him. It's his second home. A situation my Auntie Madge, longstanding rugby widow, accepts with her usual amused tolerance. 'Let the old bigamist have his fling,' she says. 'After all he's been married to the rugby club far longer than he's been married to me.'

So now, most days, summer and winter, that's where you'll find Uncle R attending to his duties at the Mellstock rugby club's HQ. Occasionally, weather permitting, he can be seen taking the air in a deckchair in the lee of the building or on the verandah.

But most of the time he's busy doing not very much inside his beloved pavilion. Eagerly awaiting and ever hoping to welcome callers. And of course, polishing up half a century of memories with which to regale them. For if there's one thing he likes more than just being there, it's being there with someone to talk rugby to.

Which is where I come in – literally. For, much to his delight (although he'd never admit it) I'm now in the Mellstock first side. And he is after all, my favourite uncle. So, in addition to all my normal playing and training visits to the ground, I've taken to dropping in at other times as well. On my way home from work in the evening. Sunday mornings. Saturday lunchtimes in the summer.

The ritual is always the same. He pulls a couple of his best pints. We settle down to have what he calls a natter. And I sit back and get ready to enjoy myself as Uncle R remembers the funny side of rugby.

Chapter 2

A New Season

It was mid August. A Friday. We were getting ready for the new season. I was recuperating on the bar sofa after my third, solo, keep-fit session in as many days. Uncle R was tapping the last of three new barrels ready for the start of official club training the following afternoon.

A scorching, sultry day was turning into a sweltering evening. Thunder grumbled on the horizon. Inside the Mellstock pavilion the mouldy odour of a hundred years of rugby-past was particularly strong. The atmosphere in the bar positively suffocating. As Uncle R had described it earlier with what, for him, passed as wit, 'So close – it's almost touchin'.'

From my resting place under the window I regarded my favourite relative across the room. He was holding a sample glass of the new brew up to the rays of the dying sun. And sqinting at it with his practical, piercing, cockerel eye.

'Clear as maiden's water,' he announced, taking a small sip. 'Cool as an Eskimo's lunch-box.' He emptied the glass. 'And smooth as a vestal virgin's thigh.' He smacked his wet, wine-red, pipe-smoker's lips lasciviously.

'Yes, Unk, but is it worth drinking?'

I ducked to avoid the beer mat that came sailing my way.

'Saucy little bugger. Liquid gold. That's what that is. Cream of the crop. Amber nectar if I ever tasted it. Fit for the Queen of England. Brenda herself. Ignoramus. I got a good mind to close the bar now. And leave you gaspin'. That'd larn you. You little toe-rag.'

I fell to my knees and clasped my hands in supplication. 'Don't do it Unk,' I cried piteously. 'Is that the way to reward a good servant who's sweated his guts out three nights on the trot, for the greater glory of the Mellstock RFC? Is that the way to treat a poor sod so dehydrated he's crippled with cramp and coughing up fag ends? I throw myself on your mercy. As the Irishman said to his chiropodist – 'Me fate is in your hands'.'

I sank down and buried my head in the sofa cushions.

Uncle R was not particularly amused.

'Silly sod,' he said, pulling me a pint and plonking it down on the counter. 'Stop pissin' about and drink that. I got a bone to pick with you.'

I got up and settled myself on a bar stool.

'Bone, Unk? What bone? What have I done now?'

He levelled one suspicious, fowl-like eye directly at me.

'Three nights runnin' you bin here trainin'. And official club trainin' don't start 'til tomorrow. What are you up to, Rich? Lazy young sod like you. Comin' here all on your tod and deliberately runnin' yourself into the ground. You must have a reason. Hidden agenda, as you like to call it. So come on, what's going on?'

I looked at him in astonishment.

'Up to, Unk? Hidden agenda, Unk? Going on? Are you barmy? I've absolutely no idea what you're talking about. I'm not up to anything, I assure you. And nothing's going on – except training.'

He pulled a long face, flared his nostrils and looked sceptical.

'You tellin' me you aren't gettin' ready to turn professional? Haven't been got at by one of them talent scout buggers from Saracens, Harlequins, London bloody Irish, or some other kiss-me-ass, so-called top class club like that? That what you're sayin'? Nobody's made you an offer you can't refuse? I don't believe it.'

He glared at me.

I shook my head sadly.

'Unk, I've warned you before about the Brasso. A couple of cans of that and it's blast off. You're in orbit. DTs. Hallucinations. The lot. These voices in your head. Telling you about the top clubs being after me. They're not real, you know. Just figments of your poor old, metal-polish-befuddled mind. Shame really. I'd love to be courted by Sarries or the Quins. But no such luck. So I guess I'll have to make do with good old reliable, Minor League South, Mellstock.' Once again he wasn't particularly amused. But he was obviously relieved.

'Sarky young bastard. Takin' the P out of your old uncle like that. Show a bit of respect to your elders and betters can't you. Anyway I'm glad to hear you're not thinkin' of goin' over to the rugby leagueites. Though you can't blame me for bein' suspicious. All this sudden trainin' crap. Just not your style. Couch potato like you.'

He sniffed in disapproval, took a pull at his pint, and then gazed pointedly at my untouched glass on the counter.

'And I thought you said you were dyin' of thirst. Don't tell me you're thinkin' of signin' the pledge as well. Becoming a bleedin' White Ribboner. I couldn't bear it.'

He looked appalled.

'You aren't, are you?'

I gave him a withering glance, picked up my drink, sank it in three quick swallows, and banged the empty glass back on the counter.

'Answer your question, Unk?'

He grinned like a Chinese idol.

'Good lad,' he said, 'that's more like it. Have another on me.'

He filled our glasses.

'Here's to dear old Mellstock,' he said 'and the start of another bloody good season.'

'Hear, hear, Unk,' I replied, 'I'll drink to that.'

So we did.

Outside the evening sky was lit by a sudden flash. It was followed by what sounded like a twenty-one gun rapid salute. The rain came down as if poured from a bucket.

Uncle R went over to the window and stood for a

few moments watching it fall. Then he emptied his glass, came back, took mine, refilled both, and settled himself on the stool next to me.

'Talkin' of rain,' he said, 'did I ever tell you about my first visit to the Arms Park?'

Chapter 3

Unforgettable, Unforgotten

'It was quite a while ago now, Rich. Three Welsh national stadiums ago, in fact. Not the bloody great Millenium pleasure dome they've got now, of course. Or the one before that. But the one before that. The one that was Cardiff's ground as well. The one with the old wooden stands, and the quagmire pitch. The real Arms Park.'

Uncle R looked at me expectantly.

I looked blank.

'Sorry, Unk. But I haven't a clue what you're on about. Before my time you know. I was born in 1979, remember, not 1879.'

He gave me one of his looks.

'You've just gotta be sarky, haven't you. Can't resist comin' the old acid. Love to wrong-foot your old uncle. Well listen here, young Rich. I'm payin' you a compliment if only you knew it. Pardon me for thinkin' you might have some faint interest in a bit of genuine rugby history.'

He shook his head and turned away with a snort.

I was duly chastened.

'Begging your parsnip, Unk. Just me being stupid. Won't happen again. Promise. Scout's honour. Go on. I'm all ears.' I wiggled mine. And waggled my eyebrows.

He couldn't help laughing.

'Clown. Well, pin back your shell-likes, then, and listen. You never know, you might learn somethin'. I'm talkin' about forty years ago. 1959. Our unbeaten season. One of the best years Mellstock ever had. And largely due to one man. Chap called Dai Davies...'

'Welshman by any chance, Unk?' It was out before I could stop myself. 'Oh God, Unk. Sorry. Sorry. Sorry.' I lifted both hands in a peace sign. And waited for the explosion.

It didn't come. Instead he groaned, raised his eyes to the ceiling and sought divine assistance.

'Dear God. Give me strength. Stay thy servant's hand so that it don't accidentally slip and catch this cheeky young sod a fourpenny one right across the chops. But warn him, Lord, that if he interrupts me just once more, he'll get the toe of my right winklepicker RIGHT UP HIS JUVENILE JAXI.'

He smiled sweetly and resumed his discourse.

'Now where was I. Ah yes – Dai Davies. Outstandin' stand-off he was. Quick. Jink off either foot. Lovely outside break. Beautiful kicker of the ball. Wonderful hands. Class act all round. He's the one who took me to the Arms Park that year. He worshipped the place. And particularly the Welsh spectators. Nothin' to touch them anywhere else in the world, he said. And he was right.

'You'd have loved that day, Rich. Yes. Even an unfeelin' little turd like you. You'd have been affected by that atmosphere. Just like I was. Yes. I know you think I'm a sentimental old twat who lives in the past. And maybe you're right. But that day in some ways, was better than anythin' I've ever experienced on a rugby ground before or since. I'll never forget it if I live to be a hundred. And don't say that only gives me another couple of years, or I'll have yours for garters. All right?

'January 17th, 1959, it was. Wales against England. And it rained all bloody day. A bit like this evenin'. Only without the fireworks. Bloke called Roberts. From Pontyberem. Pal of Dai's. Got us the tickets. And promised to get us into the Cardiff clubhouse after the game. We rendezvoused with him in a pub called The Black Ram, somewhere out in the Cardiff suburbs, at eleven o' clock. The back bar, he said. He was already there when we arrived. He and half the local rugby club. Three of whom. His party. Had cornered one end of the bar. Short, squat chap he...'

A sound like a gasometer exploding obliterated what he was saying. And a million-volt searchlight lit up the bar for a few seconds. The thunderstorm had just about reached its peak.

Uncle R gave in gracefully. 'Can't fart against that lot Rich,' he said, as he slid from his stool and vanished behind the bar in search of liquid stiffeners. When he returned he handed me a fresh pint, took a long pull at his own, and continued his tale.

'Short, squat chap he was. Mr Roberts of Pontyberem. Built like a brick outhouse. And impeccably dressed in Welsh tweeds, flat cap and navy blue British Warm. Front row forward written all over him.

'He introduced us to his colleagues. They were all called Roberts. "Pleased to meet you" they said. "Bass or Worthington ?" And distributed pints all round.

"Iechyd da. First to-day," they announced. And proceeded to down their drinks in one long, unbroken swallow.

"Lovely pint," they added, placin' their glasses neatly on the bar counter, and smackin' their lips in unison. "Same again?" And before we could say No, Dai and I found ourselves with a second large beer awaitin' our attention.

'And so it went on Rich. Pints all the way. Right across the city. As, one after the other, we visited the back, front, side, public, private and saloon bars of six pubs on a direct line from the Black Ram to the famous Angel Hotel in downtown Cardiff.

'By this time I felt that one more "lovely pint" and I'd Yacky dah my breakfast all over the floor of the Angel's so-called cocktail bar. But fortunately for me I wasn't put to the test. Dai's bloody stupid, macho attitude to rugby saved me from that.

'It was one of his daft ideas that real rugby men never watched a match sittin' down. Silly bugger. Which is why the four Mr Roberts had reserved stand seats and were able to stay at the Angel for a snack lunch and a further hour's drinkin'. While we poor idiots had to make our way to the ground there and then, to make sure we got a decent spot from which to see the game standin' up.

'So, with an hour and a quarter still to go to kick-off, we set out in the drivin' rain to find the "unreserved standin" queue.'

'It didn't take long. The Welsh aren't like us, Rich. They've got a proper sense of sportin' priorities. The Arms Park is bang in the centre of Cardiff. Rather as though Twickenham were in Piccadilly. We were in the queue in five minutes and inside Dai's dream ground in twenty.'

'I can't say I was over-impressed when I got there. Maybe it was the rain. Maybe it was the drink. But it all seemed a bit seedy, run-down and dreary to me. And then there was the thing that looked like a blinkin' dog-racin' track, runnin' all the way round the pitch, complete with overhead lightin'. That certainly came as a bit of a surprise. On top of which, the whole place ponged a bit of fag-ends and stale beer.

'Not that Dai seemed to mind. Happy as a sandboy in the steady downpour, he led me round the pitch to the North Terracin'. It was in a sort of long, slopin' cavern underneath the North Stand. We bagged a spot right at the front and to one side. "Plum position" Dai explained. "In the dry. Good view. And near the bogs."

'We took advantage of those straightaway. A wise move as it turned out. Within half an hour we were engulfed in a vast crowd of Welshmen, singin', shoutin', stampin', cheerin', laughin'. And all smellin' strongly of squashed leeks.

'On the pitch, a group of lads were makin' all sorts of lewd gestures with a large, green, cardboard, imitation of their national vegetable. While behind them the band of the Welsh Guards marched up and down and played songs from the shows.

*Lewd gestures with a large,
green cardboard imitation of their national vegetable.*

'And the Welshmen sang. Not necessarily the same songs as the band was playin'. But whatever took their fancy in the part of the ground they happened to be. Our lot were into hymns. And they really hammered them out, Rich. I was quite impressed. And began to get an inklin' of what Dai meant about the special atmosphere of the place. For there's no doubt about it. When it comes to rugby, there's definitely no crowd like a Welsh crowd. And when it comes to Welsh crowds, there's definitely no Welsh crowd like a Welsh crowd at the Arms Park on an international day. Especially when they all get together and sing Land of my Fathers. By God, Rich, that's really somethin' else altogether.

'It came a few minutes before kick-off. A bloke in a blue raincoat plodded slowly across the field, his footprints fillin' up with rain behind him. He stepped onto a small, portable, wooden rostrum in the middle of the pitch, and bowed in turn to all four corners of the stadium. The crowd roared. He lifted his arms. The crowd fell silent. The bandsmen raised their instruments. The crowd held it breath. His arms fell. And they started.

'I cried, Rich. Don't ask me why. I don't know why. But it was just so... so bloody marvellous. All those people. All those Welshmen. Singin' their hearts out. For Wales. For rugby. And for victory on that muddy, bloody field, against the old enemy.

'I knew then exactly what Dai meant when he insisted there was no other place like it in the whole of the rugby world. And I agree with him. What was it old Rupert Brooke said, Rich? Yes. Rupert Brooke. The bloke from Grantchester. Don't look so bloody surprised. I did learn a bit of poetry at school. I'm not a complete thicko. Like some I could mention.

'"Unforgettable. Unforgotten." That's what he said, Rich. Unforgettable. Unforgotten. And that's exactly how I feel about it still. All those Taffies. All those years ago. Land of my Fathers.'

He leaned on the bar and gazed into space. Eyes full of the past. Across the room a bee suddenly buzzed and banged angrily at the window before escaping into the dying storm. But he neither saw nor heard it. He was back with fifty thousand Welshmen singing in the rain on a dark winter day in Cardiff. And crying with the rest of them for the joy and passion of it all.

I gave him a minute or two, and then gently broke into his reverie.

'What about the game then, Unk? What was that like?'

I prepared myself for another sizeable slab of geriatric nostalgia. But, as ever, he surprised me.

'Bloody awful,' he said. 'Absolutely bloody awful. Not the players' fault. The rain beat everybody. Complete bloody mud bath. After ten minutes you couldn't tell one side from the other. The Welsh won. Five – love. But they were lucky.'

'The crowd didn't half sing when Dewi Bebb scored their try in the first half, and Terry Davies knocked over the conversion. And they sang even louder, just before the end, when Risman scored the equaliser, right by the posts, and the so-and-so Irish referee disallowed it. But there's no gettin' away from it. As a game of rugby it was a really scrappy bloody affair.

'Not that Dai minded. He was ecstatic at the finish. Everyone else had stopped singin' by then. And were clappin', cheerin', and tryin' to get onto the pitch. But he just stood there. Arms above his head. Fists clenched. Eyes glazed. Starin' like a madman up into the rain. Bawlin' on and on about the land of his fathers. Singin' completely out of tune. And annoyin' everybody within ten yards of us.'

'And after the match, Unk. What happened then?

Did you manage to get into the Cardiff clubhouse?'

'We certainly did, Rich. And bloody interestin' it was too. But before I tell you about that let's have a drop more neck oil.'

Chapter 4

The MWOB Museum

The thunderstorm was dying out. Slipping away to the west. Grumbling and flickering. Leaving a clean blue sky and the glaring remnants of a fiery sunset.

Having produced a fresh supply of neck oil, Uncle R stood at the window of the Mellstock pavilion surveying the sodden ground and packing his pipe. Thumbing down the last shreds of a fill of Erinmore, he flared the charred bowl of his favourite bulldog briar with his old gas, flame-thrower, lighter, and puff, puff, puffed the tobacco into flame. A stream of silver smoke, aromatic as bruised thyme, drifted across the room. Grunting contentedly, he came back to the bar, settled himself on his stool, picked up his untouched pint, and prepared to finish his half-told tale.

'As I was sayin', the trouble with Dai was that he wouldn't stop singin'. Pumped up by the beer, the game and the crowd, he went on and on about the land of his fathers in that tone-deaf bloomin' voice of his, until the spectators shufflin' off the North Terracin' around us were so cheesed off, they told him to put a sock in it. Which he did. Although even then, all the way to the Cardiff Athletic clubhouse in the corner of the ground, he kept on mutterin' under his breath somethin' that sounded like "My Hen Had The Bad Eye", to his own tuneless version of the Welsh national anthem.

'When we finally got there, Mr Roberts of Pontyberem and his relatives had already arrived. Part of a group of about fifty Welshmen. All trying to get in. In front of them a huge man in the uniform of the Corps of Commissionaires barred the door.

"We're all members," they shouted.

"Show us your tickets, then," he shouted back.

"Lost in the post," they bawled.

"Pull the other one," he bawled back.

"Come on," they implored, "be a pal."

"Not tonight Josephine," he grinned, "I got a headache."

"Mean sod," they complained, "get the Secretary."

"Can't," he replied flatly.

"Why not?"

"He's over at the Angel with the Big Five," he announced in his best, imitation, cut-glass English accent. "They're havin' tea and crumpets with the President of the Har Heff Yew." He cackled. "Why not nip over and join 'em?" The crowd fell to muttering. Mr Roberts moved in. The commissionaire leaned a large, cauliflower ear down to him.

'Into it, Mr Roberts passed some whispered comment. The guardian removed one of his white gloves. He and Mr Roberts shook hands warmly. The commissionaire smiled, nodded, and put his glove back on again.

'"VIPs from England," he bawled, salutin' us as

we passed into the building. The crowd howled. The commissionaire silenced them with a warning wave of his white-gloved hand. The door closed behind us and we heard no more.'

Uncle R paused. The demands of his dramatic monologue had taken their temporary toll. His throat was dry, and his pipe had gone out. He took a long pull at his glass. Completed the reaming, emptying, stem-cleaning, filling, tamping, singeing, sucking, puffing, re-lighting ritual of his pipe. And after a few quick draws, continued his story.

'I dunno what the Cardiff Athletic clubhouse is like these days, Rich. I've never been back since that original visit. But as I remember it then, it was quite a swish place for a rugby pavilion. Brick-built, two-storey, sizeable, with a billiard-room downstairs and a great big long bar on the first floor, overlookin' of all things a cricket field. Walls covered with team photos. Hundreds of famous names. And a bloody great Springbok head on the wall behind the bar to remind you that in 1907 Cardiff beat the South African tourin' side.

'Mr Roberts of Pontyberem had us up the stairs and into the bar like spit off a shovel. And soon we were wedged into a packed crowd of Welshmen all drinkin' pints of Brains bitter and talkin' rugby.

'Perhaps all rugby discussions in the Cardiff bars after an international game, even today, end up at some time talkin' about the Wales-All Blacks match of 1905. I wouldn't be at all surprised. Anyway, about three pints later, ours with the Roberts clan certainly did.

'Yes, I know you think it's bloody ridiculous,

Rich. A lot of old fuddy-duddies maunderin' on about a game that took place fifty-odd years earlier. Nearly a century ago now. Geriatric farts in their second childhood, borin' everyone in sight with long-winded accounts of players you've never heard of. But you're wrong.

'Don't worry. I'm not goin' to tell you the story of that 1905 match now. But I will one day. Because despite what you think, I reckon you'll find it fascinatin'. Wait and see. For the moment though, let's just say that on that day in 1959, in the bar of the Cardiff Athletic clubhouse, Dai, I and the four Mr Roberts's, were happily discussin' the historic try, and the man who not only scored it, but helped to stop the New Zealanders from gettin' the equaliser in the second half.

'His name won't mean anythin' to you of course. Ignorant little bleeder that you are. But mention Teddy Morgan – Dr Teddy Morgan of Guy's Hospital, London Welsh and Wales – to any Welshman, or to anyone else who knows anythin' at all about the oval ball game, and they'll sit up and take notice.

'Anyway, we were talkin' about him. "The fastest rugby sprinter in the world" as one eminent Welsh selector called him at the time. And arguin' whether his was the most famous try ever scored in rugby.

'As the only Englishman in the group, I was pluggin' the second of Alex Obolensky's two tries for England against the All Blacks at Twickenham in 1936? Prince Alex Obolensky by the way, he was, Rich. A genuine, bleedin' Russian Prince. But you won't know about him either, will you? Ignoramus that you are.

'Anyway, I was pressin' his claim. Because a lot of people would say that that second score of his was one of rugby's classic tries of all time. A lot of people Rich. But not Dai and the Roberts clan. Not compared with Teddy Morgan's. No way. I was just fightin' off their jeers and howls of derision, when a chap standin' right next to us suddenly poked his oar into our discussion.

'"We got his jersey downstairs," he said. "The one he was wearing when he scored that try."

'Teddy Morgan's jersey'.

'I looked at him in astonishment Rich. Couldn't believe my ears. 'You've got Prince Obolensky's jersey,' I said 'here in Cardiff?' He looked disgusted. "Nah. Course not. Not his. Teddy Morgan's. Whose d'you think? Go and have a look at it. It's down on the ground floor. In one of the showcases in the billiard room. What the committee calls the Archive, and we call the MWOB Museum. Men With Oval Balls. Get it?" He hooted with laughter, banged me on the shoulder, and turned back to his companions.

'So of course, we went down, Rich. Dai and I and Mr R of Ponty B, that is. The others preferred to remain drinkin'.

'I was expectin' to see a typical collection of rude, rugby club paraphernalia, Rich. You know the sort of thing we've got here, only better. Doctored road signs. Lock's Bottom. Wookey's Hole. This Bay (Boy) Reserved For The Vicar. Stuff like that. Ladies' black French knickers, framed and labelled "In memory of those who've gone beyond". And a motley collection of false teeth, trusses, wooden legs and suchlike. But that wasn't it at all.

'In the billiard room two older club members were enjoyin' a quiet game of snooker.

"Is this the rugby archive?" We asked.

"Some call it that," they said, grinnin'.

"And what do you call it? Don't tell us. MWOB Museum. Right?"

They nodded.

"Mind if we take a shufti?" we asked.

"Be our guests," they said, settlin' down to their game again. So we started to look round. What a place Rich. Talk about Aladdin's cave. The collection in the glass cases all around that bare old billiard parlour was fabulous, Rich. That's the only word for it. Fabulous. The stuff of rugby legends. Livin' history. Treasure trove. A genuine memorial chapel to the oval ball game.

'I was fascinated. So were Dai and Mr Roberts. That was obvious. Mr R was hardly drinkin' at all. And old Dai, primed with three pints of Brain's best, was floatin' in some beery seventh heaven all on his own.

'We looked at silk touch flags sixty or seventy years old. Tasselled caps presented by internationals dead these fifty years. Ancient, shapeless, leather balls from famous old matches. Programmes and photos by the score. And a wonderful collection of jerseys of visiting clubs from every level of the game, and from dozens of the most oustanding individual players of three-quarters of a century.

'It was magic, Rich. Real magic. And then we came to IT. Teddy Morgan's jersey. The very one he was wearin' when he scored the historic try. It was in a glass case all to itself. Preserved like a quail in aspic. And to me in my half-slewed state, still givin' off a faint whiff of that original, sweet, sweaty, smell of success.

'It was a great moment. I was touched. But as for Dai, it was just too much for him to bear. Maudlin already from a day of almost non-stop boozin', the sight of the old hero's muddy jersey made him really flip his lid.

'He tried to speak to me. "Ronnie, bach," he mumbled in a choked voice that had suddenly become as Welsh as Owen Glendwr squared. "Ronnie bach...

iss wunnerful... abslooly bloody wunnerful. Ronnie... Ronnie... ole fren... my cub runneth over..." And he burst into loud wails.

'Mr Roberts was also clearly moved. I could tell that at once. For a full two minutes his pint of Brains lay cradled in the crook of his arm completely untouched. And when finally he did manage to take a short pull at it, it seemed to bring on a chokin' fit that caused him to trumpet into his handkerchief for ages.'

Uncle R paused briefly to fill our glasses. When he went on it was with a catch in his voice that could have been a sob, but sounded suspiciously like a giggle.

'As I said, Rich, it was a touchin' moment. And I make no bones about it. I was – affected.'

He paused again.

'And so, obviously were the snooker players. "Excuse me," the older of the two said, noddin' towards the wailin' Dai and the trumpetin' Mr Roberts. "But could you ask them to do that outside? We got a match on here."

Chapter 5

Looking for Dr Morgan

Uncle R stopped talking, got down from his stool and was moving towards the bar door. Flaked out on the old sofa by the window, on to which I had collapsed while he was getting us fresh pints, I enquired mildly whether that was the end of his Arms Park story.

'Finished a bit sudden-like, ain't it, Unk? Or is this one of those avante garde efforts where you make up your own ending to suit yourself? Sort of Sam Beckett, Harold Pinter stuff?'

He stopped, looked back and grinned at me.

'Who do they play for?' he said 'Bedlam Rovers?' Anyway, young Rich, keep your shorts on, the yarn's not over yet. We're just havin' a bit of a dramatic pause so to speak. Private Patients' Plan, you might say – Pee Pee Pee, get it?' He cackled. 'And while I'm out there havin' a word with the vicar, I thought I might as well bring a new barrel on stream. Don't want essential services bein' interrupted do we? Shouldn't take me more than ten minutes even at my age.' He cackled again. 'You can spend the time lookin' at one of your nice picture books while I'm away. There's an old copy of "Girls on Top" behind the bar.'

He cackled for the third time, waggled his hips

and closed the door.

I lay back, sipped my beer and decided to rest my eyes for a moment. Outside, the evening left by the storm was soft and damp. Inside, the atmosphere in the bar was warm and still. Slowly and gently I slid into the waiting arms of Morpheus.

He stirred me with the toe of his boot.

'Hey. Sleepin' Beauty. Comfortable are we? Can I fetch you something? Peeled grape? Stuffed olive? Canna pee? Fourpenny one round the ear?'

He toed me again rather more firmly.

I opened my eyes, Sighed. Stretched. Yawned. And looked at my watch.

'No thanks, Unk. Nice of you to offer. But no thanks. I might rise to another pint in due course. But meanwhile I'm looking forward to hearing the end of your story. As you can see I've been lying here literally quivering with expectation ever since you pee pee peed off half an hour ago.'

I smiled sweetly.

He sniffed and gazed heavenward in disgust.

'Saucy little toerag. You know what you need, don't you?'

'Yes, vicar,' I interjected, 'a nice winkle-picker up the jaxi. Which no doubt you'll be only too pleased to provide in due course. But perhaps we could leave that till a bit later on. After you've finished your sermon.'

He couldn't help laughing.

'Cheeky sod. I've a good mind to call 'time' and close down the bar. But you'd only go off to sleep again, and ruin a damn good story. So let's get on with it. Now where was I? Ah yes. The Arms Park. 1959. Mr Roberts of Pontyberem getting over the vapours. Dai Davies havin' an attack of boozer's gloom.

'The trouble was that outside the Cardiff clubhouse that night it was a bit nippy. Which, instead of soberin' Dai up, made him worse. Even more of a wet brewer's fart than before. And by the time we got him back to the Black Ram he was so far gone he kept tryin' to get into his car via the boot.

'That's what settled it. There was no way we were gonna let him drive. So, between us the Roberts clan and I wrapped him up like a bleedin' mummy in his car rug, strapped him into the passenger seat of his car, and I had to drive both of 'em back to Mellstock. He was out cold most of the way and when we got to his house was still half-cut. So it was no trouble keepin' him in the rug and givin' him the old fireman's lift straight into his bunk to sleep it off.

'And that would have been the end of that as far as my visit to the old Arms Park is concerned, Rich. We talk about never forgetting great days like that, but somehow we always do. Given time. And sure as eggs is eggs, Cardiff, Teddy Morgan and the historic try would have been on their way down the Swanee if Dai hadn't gone to Norfolk a few weeks later.

'The old Welsh wizard, you see, worked for the Forestry Commission. And he had to go and look at some new plantin' scheme they had goin', somewhere up around a place called North Walsham.

'He'd only been gone a couple of days when to my surprise one evenin' he was on the blower to me gibberin' like a blue-assed baboon.

'"Ronnie," he screeched, 'Ronnie bach. It's bloody incredible. Abso-bloody-lutely amazin'. You'll never believe it. What I've just been told. Never. Not in a month of Sundays boyo. D'you know what? He's here Ronnie. Right here. Here of all places. Would you Adam and Eve it. I couldn't believe my ears. I still can't get..."

'I was forced to shout him down. "Dai, hang on a minute. Calm down. Take it gently. I can't understand a bleedin' word you're sayin' old mate. Easy now. Take your time. Who's where? And where's here?"

'He groaned. "For heaven's sake Ronnie. Him. Teddy Morgan. He's here, I tell you. Right here in North Walsham. Where I'm stayin'. In this pub. The Norfolk Arms. He's here. You wouldn't credit it, would you?"

'He was right. I couldn't credit it. "Teddy Morgan, Dai. You're tellin' me Teddy Morgan's in North Walsham stayin' with you in a local pub. I should cocoa. He must be gettin' on for ninety."

'He groaned even louder. "No. No. Ronnie. I'm stayin' in the pub. Teddy died. The landlord's just told me so. Only five minutes ago. Get a bloody grip, will you. Pull your finger out, laddie."

'I was goin' to ask him if he really meant that Dr Morgan had passed over only five minutes previously. But decided not to make him any more excited than he already was.

'"Sorry Dai," I said apologetically, 'I'm afraid I'm being a bit of a dumbo here, so perhaps you wouldn't mind startin' all over again and explainin' what exactly it is you're tryin' to say to me.'

'So he did. And gradually I got the whole story out of him.

'This was it.

'On his second night at the Norfolk Arms he wandered into the residents' lounge for a pre-dinner snifter and the landlord insisted on standin' him a large G and T on the house.

'They got talkin' of course and before Dai could say "Stanley Matthews" mine host was givin' him GBH of the earhole on the subject of local soccer.

'Not that this surprised him. The walls of the pub were plastered with photographs of the local football club and the landlord was in most of 'em.

'But twenty minutes of non-stop round ball chat was too much even for kindly old Dai and he had to come clean that he was an oval ball addict who knew sweet Football Association about soccer, which wasn't really his bag anyway.

'The landlord was disappointed of course. But not so disappointed as to let a captive listener off the hook.

'"Oh, so you're a rugby man," he said "Well maybe you knew the international who used to live around these parts. Over near Mundesley I believe. I never knew him personally. But some of my customers did. And they thought a lot of him. He was a GP, see. Bloody good doctor they said. And a bloody good rugby player too in his younger days. They were always talkin' about some famous match donkey's years ago. In Wales I think it was. He scored the winnin' try apparently. Doubt if you'd remember him. Long before your time of course. Chap called…'

'At which point apparently, Dai frightened the life out of him with a bloody great shriek that stopped him dead in his tracks.

'"Don't tell me. Don't tell me." He bawled. "I just can't believe it. It was Dr Teddy Morgan wasn't it? Wasn't it?"

'The landlord was a bit shaken but kept his cool.

'"Well um, yes actually I suppose it was,' he said. 'Certainly his surname was Morgan and his Christian name, Edward. Friend of yours, was he?"

'But Dai had gone. Off his bar stool and out of the room like a long dog. To phone me of course.

'And by the time we got things straight between us, I was almost as excited as he was.

'"Well done Dai, you old bugger. Wonderful news. Now try to find out exactly where he's buried and if humanly possible get some photographs of the grave. I'll see you the minute you get back to Mellstock."

'He was completely manic by this time. God knows what the landlord must have thought.

'"Aye, aye skipper," he bawled, 'Och aye the noo and splice the mainbrace. There's gonna be a hot time in the old town tonight. Yes siree." '

'As he rang off there was the unmistakable sound of a lovesick grampus callin' to his mate. He was singing.

'But not so when he called to see me a few days later. He hadn't been able to find the grave.

'"After we talked on the phone" he moaned, I had another word with the landlord and he suggested

Teddy might be buried four or five miles away in Mundesley, near where he'd lived. Possibly in the same grave as his first wife who, he thought, had died quite a few years before he did. So I went over there. Bugger all. Not a sign of either of 'em anywhere. And virtually the same again when I had a quick look round the cemetery in North Walsham.

"I even went to the Town Council offices. The chap in the Records Office there turned out to be a rugby man himself. Played for Norwich for nearly twenty years. He got out the burial registers for the whole of the 1930s and 40s and we went through 'em together.

'Only Mrs Morgan we found was a Lydia Morgan. Died in 1936. He gave me the plot number in the town cemetery. I was sure it was Teddy's wife. But not on your Nellie. Right name. Wrong Mrs Morgan.

"And that's it, Ronnie. There was nothin' else I could think of doin'. And I'd run out of time anyway. So what the hell do we do now? Pack it in and forget it. Or try and think of some other place to look?"

'My first inclination, Rich, was to say "give up" and leave it at that. But the old sod sounded so depressed, I decided I must do something to try to cheer him up a bit.

'"Pack it in bollocks," I said. "We can't do that. Can't leave old Teddy lyin' in some unmarked grave. He's a Welsh hero. And you honour heroes. Not forget 'em. So just you leave it to me. I'll go up to North Walsham myself and make a few more enquiries. I got a cousin in Norfolk. Lives over near

Holt. He'll put me up for a couple of nights. I'll give him a ring."

'Cousin Arthur turned out to be quite useful. "Have you tried the other main church in North Walsham?' he asked. 'Not the big one in the centre, but a smaller one a bit further out. Well known for its choir. Vicar mad on music. Always puttin' on concerts. Can't remember it's name. But it's just the place that might have appealed to a Welsh doctor and his family. Why not give it a go?"

'So I did. Drove over to North Walsham. And found it almost immediately. At first, in the dim light inside, I thought the place was empty. But then I caught sight of the old lady. She was sittin' all on her own in a front pew. I sat myself down next to her and asked if the vicar was anywhere about. 'She gave me a vague look. "No," she said. "Curate?" I enquired.

"No," she said.

"No-one at all?"

"Yes," she said. "Me. I do the flowers here every other Friday."

"Ah," I said. "And you are?"

"Mrs Gotobed. I'm a widow."

"Oh. And you know the church well, obviously?"

"Should do. Been coming here for over sixty years now."

'That long eh? You didn't ever have a chap in the congregation called Teddy Morgan I suppose? A local doctor?'

'She gave me a long-sufferin' look.

"Course we did. He was my doctor. Wonderful man. He's dead now, you know."

"Yes, I know. And I'm tryin' to find out where he's buried. That's what I want to see the vicar about."

"Well, why didn't you say so. He's buried here. In the churchyard."

"Really." My heart leapt, Rich. "You don't know where exactly, I suppose?"

"No." She shook her head. "Not exactly. But he's here somewhere. You'll have to ask the Senior Church Warden exactly where. There are a lot of graves out there. But he'll know. Oh yes. He'll know all right."

'She nodded her head sagely.

"And his name, Mrs Gotobed?"

'She looked at me. Her eyes vacant.

"Whose name?"

"The Senior Church Warden's, Mrs Gotobed. The man who knows where Dr Morgan's buried."

"Oh, him," she said. "Why, Mr Turkentine of course. Or is it – Mr Waterfall? I can never remember. Anyway, he'll know."

"Thank you, Mrs Gotobed. Thank you very much. And you don't happen to know where I might find him do you?"

"Who?"

"The Senior Church Warden. You know. Mr Turkentine. Or Mr Waterfall."

"Oh, him. No. Sorry. He isn't here today. But you can leave a message if you like. There's pen and paper in the vestry. And I'll be seeing him on Sunday."

"That's very kind. Mr Turkentine you say?"

"Yes. Or Mr Waterfall. You'd better address your note to both."

'I did as she said and drove back to tell Cousin Arthur 'Bingo'-we seemed to have hit the target bang in the bull's-eye first go.

Uncle R stopped talking again, got down from his stool and moved towards the bar door for the second time in twenty minutes. He didn't go willingly. But couldn't ignore my special pleading. "P P P," I had announced, waving my empty tankard in the air, "Perfect Pint Please, Unk."

When he came back I noticed he'd filled his own two-pint pot as well. But that didn't stop him from complaining.

'Now then, not another peep outta you until I finish the story. OK? Or I'll have you off that sofa like spit off a shovel. And my toe up your fundament before you can say Oscar Wilde. Right?'

"Right, Unk. Guaranteed. Not even a whisper. Brownies' honour." I crossed my heart, gave him the two-fingered Scouts' salute and lay back on my cushions.

He couldn't quite smother his grin as he went on.

'Back in Mellstock Dai was over the moon as we waited for a word from Mr Turkentine/Waterfall. It arrived three weeks later, scribbled on a telegram form.

"Your message via Mrs Gotobed received stop," it said. "Church records searched for period you mention stop. Last Morgan died 1929 stop. Ezekiel stop. No burials in churchyard since 1930 stop. Mrs G now 96 stop. Mind gone stop. Sorry stop." It was signed "Nelson Monument, Senior Church Warden."

'To say that I was disappointed Rich, is a bit like

suggestin' that King Arthur was a bit peeved to hear that Guinevere was havin' it off with Lancelot. But since neither Dai nor I had a blind idea what to do next we decided to do nothing, bite on the bullet and hope something might turn up. And sure enough, a couple of months later, it did.

'The man in the Records Office in North Walsham wrote out of the blue, to tell us that he'd turned up the name and address of Teddy Morgan's step-daughter in the West Country and was passin' it on "in case we might think it worthwhile contacting her".

'I wrote at once and got a long letter back from the lady's brother, also a local GP, who obviously admired Teddy Morgan tremendously. "Scratch golfer," he said. "County cricketer for Glamorgan." And "once bowled out the great WG himself."

'But as for the joint grave, he couldn't help. He'd always thought it was at Mundesley. And if it wasn't, he hadn't got a clue where it might be. "Had we contacted the vicar there?"

'And God help me, Rich, I suddenly realised we hadn't. So post haste, I dashed off yet another note. And again got a reply from someone else. Mundesley vicar passed my enquiry to Trunch (a nearby village) rector. And Trunch rector's suggestion was to contact St Faith's Crematorium in Norwich. Because "Dr Morgan might have been cremated, and if so they might know what happened to the ashes."

'After goin' up so many blind alleys, Rich, I've gotta admit I didn't expect much joy from St Faith's. But this time I was wrong. They turned up trumps big time.

'I was havin' a late breakfast about a week later, when I got a call from a very tight-assed soundin' female. "Re your enquiry regarding Dr Edward Morgan" she announced, all prisms and prunes, "he died on the 1st September 1949 at the age of 68. He was cremated at St Faith's on September 3rd, and his ashes were handed to the funeral director to be taken to...."

'And then, I'll swear just for devilment, she paused for a few seconds before tellin' me where.

'It was, as we'd all thought, to Mundesley. And Teddy and his first wife, as we'd all thought too, are buried together. But not in the churchyard.

'The ashes of both of 'em – sixteen years apart – were scattered in the sea off the Mundesley coast.

'The search was over, Rich. It'd taken us nearly six months. But we'd finally cracked it. And boy was I delighted? I'll say I was. Not so much for myself. But for good old Dai.

'You should have seen him when I gave him the news. Slapped me on the back till I could hardly stand. Bear-hugged me half to death. Danced me round the room. Kissed me on both cheeks. Called me "A Bloody Wonder." Bought me three pints in a row. Had a bit of a cry. And vowed that through his relatives, and people like Mr Roberts of Pontyberem, he'd spread the news far and wide throughout the whole of Wales.

'Whether he did or not, I've no idea. Maybe it was common knowledge there anyway. But I'll never know that either. Not now. Dai left Mellstock about nine months later. And I lost touch with him a long time ago.

'But just before he left the town, at his farewell booze-up at the rugby club, I presented him with a special memento of his time in Mellstock. It was a picture postcard of Mundesley Bay taken on a sunny day from the little patch of grass with a seat on it at the top of the steps down to the beach, opposite the Seaview House Hotel. I got my Cousin Arthur to send me two. I've still got the other one.

'And every year, Rich, when December 16th comes around, I fish it out and cast my mind back to old Dai.

'Yes, I know what you're thinkin', unfeelin' little turd that you are. "Sentimental old git, livin' in the past as always. When's he gonna get real?"

But you don't understand. It's the anniversary of Wales's victory over the First All Blacks in 1905, you see. December 16th. The day Teddy Morgan scored the historic try.

'And that always makes me think of the marvellous day we had together at the Arms Park forty odd years ago. Me, Mr Roberts of Pontyberem and old Dai. The day Dai first saw the great man's jersey in the glass case in the MWOB museum in the Cardiff clubhouse.

'And then I have one of my little fantasies, Rich. As I look at Cousin Arthur's faded old postcard. In my mind's eye I see Dai in it. Clear as a bell. Good old hero-worshippin' Dai. Sometimes leadin' a small group of boozy Welshmen well-oiled from the Seaview House across the road. Sometimes completely on his tod. Makin' his annual pilgrimage to Mundesley. Standin' by the seat on that little patch of grass at the top of the steps leadin' down to the beach. Facin' out to sea. Fists clenched, eyes glazed, gazin' up to heaven, bellowin'"Land of my Fathers" at the top of his voice. Bellowin' it to Teddy Morgan and his wife. Out there under the waves. Lettin' 'em know they're not forgotten.

'And the fact that it's probably the worst, tone-deaf, tuneless, ear-achin' travesty of the Welsh national anthem you're ever likely to hear doesn't seem to matter a damn.'

Chapter 6

Easter In Wales

'That's somethin' else they don't have any more,' Uncle R announced suddenly from under his hat. Rousing me from a quiet drowse.

We were lying in deckchairs in the lee of the Mellstock pavilion. Resting with beer and sandwiches after a morning spent making minor repairs to the exterior of my elderly relative's favourite building.

It was early October. Indian Summer. A Sunday. Sunny but with a bite in the wind.

Old Panama hat over his eyes, stocky legs up on a cushioned footstool, arms folded contentedly over an ample paunch, my uncle lay at rest. Everything about him at ease. All faculties suspended. Except of course – as I should have guessed – his nostalgia.

'What's that, Unk?' I mumbled. 'What don't they have any more?'

He transferred the Panama from his face to his chest.

'Easter tours,' he said. 'We haven't had one for ages.'

'So what, Unk? Who cares?' I was still half asleep.

'I do, you young turd. They used to be a tradition. We had 'em every year for donkey's years. Regular as clockwork. Just like we had the KO Cup and the Fancy Dress Booze-up and Dance. But now they've gone too. They've all gone. And nobody seems to care a tuppenny damn. God help us, we haven't even had a dinner since 1998. I really dunno what this blasted club's coming to.'

He shook his head sadly. I nodded in sympathy.

'Sorry, Unk. I know how you feel. But I'm afraid you've gotta face it. Times change. Chaps aren't much interested in that sort of thing any more. They'd just as soon be down at the disco, or chatting up the tottie at the wine bar. Or over Easter, raving it up at some pop festival.'

'More fool them, then. They don't know what they're missin'. The KO Cup matches could get a bit hairy at times, I agree. But the rest were bloody good fun. Especially the Wanderers' Easter tours. Three days rugby and five days off the leash with the boys. And the local girls. Lovely. Just as good as any muddy, bloody, pop festival if you ask me.'

He raised his eyebrows like a naughty teenager and gave me a vulgar leer.

'Nothin' like endin' the season with a bang, eh, Rich? If you'll excuse my French.'

He waited for me to smile. I duly obliged.

'God, laddo, I remember one tour. To South Wales. It was the the year after I went to the Arms Park with Dai Davies. 1960 . Dai was leavin' the club at the end of that season. So they made him tour captain. Talk about puttin' the dipso in charge of the bar. What a weekend that was.'

He swallowed his beer, helped himself to a

sandwich and sat gazing into space. Obviously back in the sixties. You could almost see the long-distance, rose-coloured glasses.

It would have been akin to cruelty to dumb animals not to have joined him. So I did.

'Tell me, Unk,' I said, after a short pause, 'who did you play that time? Cardiff, Newport, Swansea, Llanelli?'

Uncle R looked pained.

'Stop tryin' to extract the old pizza, Rich. It don't become you. Anyway you know what sarcasm is, don't you? The lowest form of defecated wit. So, no. As it happens we didn't play the big four on that occasion. They'd already been signed up by the likes of the Baabaas and the Quins. But funnily enough Swandiff, Carport and Newsea hadn't. So we played them instead.'

I couldn't help grinning.

'Who's extracting what from whom now Unk? Swandiff, Carport and Newsea. You are pulling my Pilsner, aren't you?'

'Joke, Rich, joke.' He produced a big enamel jug and helped us to more beer.

'To be honest, after all this time, I can't remember the real names of the three small clubs we played. But they were such jaw-breakers that even then we couldn't pronounce them. So they became Swandiff, Carport and Newsea. And that's what they've stayed ever since.'

'Very droll, Unk. Highly subtile. But tell me. How did the Wanderers get on against those stars of the Welsh rugby firmament?'

Uncle R put his beer down on the grass. His face beamed with pleasure.

'Lying in deckchars in the lee of the Mellstock pavilion'.

'I'm glad you asked, Rich. And in a word – fabulously. It's still the best tour they've ever had. Won one, drew one, lost one. Tremendous celebrations when we got back to Mellstock. Club went mad.'

I couldn't believe my ears. Or my eyes. He was as excited as a long-dog down a rabbit hole. He might have been talking of some remarkable event of a few days past, rather than a trivial rugby victory of forty years ago.

'But Unk, what d'you mean celebrations. You won one game out of three. And you had celebrations? What were you defending? A hundred per cent beaten record?'

I laughed.

So did Uncle R.

'Exactly, Rich. That's exactly what the Wanderers were doin'. They'd never won a match before. We got the two oldest club members into the bar and asked them to think back. First one did. And then the other. Between them they covered seventy years plus. And they both agreed. They couldn't recall a single Wanderers victory in the whole of that time. So we celebrated, Rich. Loud and long. It was some night, I can tell you.'

He finished his sandwich. Took a long pull at his beer. Flopped his hat back over his eyes. And appeared to go to sleep.

I drowsed along with him for a few minutes until idle curiosity got the better of me.

'Who did you beat?' I asked him.

'Wrong,' he said from under his hat.

'What d'you mean wrong, Unk. All I said was who did you beat?'

'Right.'

'What d'you mean, Right? You said wrong.'

'You were wrong.' Uncle R still spoke from under his hat. 'It's not – Who did you beat. It's Whom did you beat. For heaven's sake, Rich. Where were you dragged up? Borstal?'

I sighed deeply.

'Stone the crows, Unk. All right then. Which team on the tour to South Wales in 1960 did the Mellstock Wanderers beat? Does that suit your majesty?'

A chuckle came from under the hat.

'Interested, are we? Well, that is interesting. I

thought I heard you say just now that – 'Chaps aren't much interested in that sort of thing any more'. Dull old crapola like Easter tours to South Wales.'

Uncle R was enjoying himself. I stifled my growing exasperation.

'Look here, Unk. Just think about it. What with telly, computers, package holidays, and all that sort of stuff. It stands to reason, doesn't it, that lots of chaps today won't be as interested as your generation was in rugby clubs and rugby club jaunts: especially jaunts that took place before they were even born.

'But, as you know very well indeed, I don't happen to be one of them. I am interested in Mellstock RFC. And Mellstock RFC's affairs. And – don't ask me why – I'm also interested, God help me, in your tales of Mellstock RFC happenings of forty and fifty years ago. So for the last time. If it's not too much trouble. Which of the three teams did you beat. Was it Swandiff, Carport, or Newsea?'

I knew I sounded like a pedantic twit. I knew that he knew it too. And I knew that he wasn't about to let it pass without rubbing my nose in it.

But as ever he surprised me.

Slowly and deliberately he removed the Panama from his face. Like some aimiable old oriental Buddha, he was grinning from ear to ear.

'OK, Rich,' he said. 'Keep your hair on. Just my little joke. Don't get your oojahs in a twist. The answer to your most interestin' question is that the 1960 Mellstock Wanderers, havin' lost their openin' game at Swandiff and drawn the second at Carport, went on to beat Newsea in the third and final match of their tour. Satisfied? And if by any chance you'd like to hear more about that historic occasion, you know very well that you only have to say the word.'

There was something irresistible in that wicked grin. Even the most righteous of indignations weren't proof against the twinkle in those saucy, little cockerel eyes of his.

Exasperation evaporated.

'OK, Unk,' I said. 'Go on then. Tell me about it.'

Chapter 7

Swandiff

Uncle R refilled my glass, topped up his tankard, adjusted the cushion on his footstool, settled back into his deckchair, and exhaled a long, self-satisfied sigh. Like a spider lazily contemplating a successfully trapped fly.

I smiled at him in amused affection.

'When I said "Tell me about it," Unk. I didn't mean tell me about all three matches in detail. I just meant I'd be interested to hear a bit more about the tour in general. OK?'

'Of course, dear boy. Of course. I understand perfectly. You want a brief account of what went on that Easter weekend. Just the highlights. Not all the borin' details. And that's exactly what you're gonna get. You know me, Rich. I don't beat about the bush. No verbal diarrhoea here. Ask me the time and I'll say it straight out. I won't tell you how to make a clock. Trust me. I'll give it you short and sweet. So take it easy, my dear fellow. Rest your bones and enjoy yourself.'

I groaned inwardly. He was being much too polite. All this Noel Coward/John Gielgud, 'dear boy', 'my dear fellow', stuff. Much too smarmy. Not his normal style at all. Unless he wanted something. And clearly what he wanted at the moment was to tell me all about that Mellstock Wanderers 1960 South Wales tour. In minute detail. It was obviously going to be a long haul. And unless I wanted to upset him, I had no alternative but to bite the bullet and listen.

'Carry on, Unk,' I said resignedly, as I lay back and prepared to think of England.

From under the floppy brim of his ancient Panama one parrot-like eye gave me a naughty wink.

'Right ho then, Rich. Let's start at the beginnin' shall we. It was a lovely mornin'. The day we left Mellstock. Mid-April weather. Clear and sunny. But with a nip in the air. Just chilly enough to call for a swift pint before we got on the bus.

'We gathered at the club here. Twenty-five players and a couple of senior members who came along for the ride and a rest from domestic bliss. We took on stores. Four light ales and four Guinness. Crates of course. And were away by ten.

'I sat up in the front with Dai. Near the booze. He was pretty pumped up about it all, I can tell you. Over the moon to be goin' back to his homeland. And tickled pink to be captain for the tour. The nearer we came to Wales, the more excited he got.

'When he realised we'd actually crossed the border somewhere near Chepstow he went quite doolally. "This is it, boyos," he bawled. Rushin' up and down the bus. Punchin' people on the shoulder. Slappin' 'em on the back. "We're here. Land of my fathers. God's own country. Bloody marvellous. How Green Was My Valley."

'It was quite touchin' really. But a bit misplaced,

Rich. We happened to be passin' through a particularly ugly industrial estate at the time.

'By the time we stopped for a liquid lunch in a pub just outside Newport, our temporary skipper had made a sizeable hole in the Guinness tryin' to get a reluctant bus to join him in a series of toasts to Wales and all things Welsh. And during the break he kept tryin' again. Only to fall foul of one of our senior members, who insisted on shoutin' out "New Zealand" every time our captain raised his pint to "The greatest rugby nation in the world."

'Finally, and much to the irritation of the landlord – a supporter of the Black and Ambers – he jumped on a chair and started singin' in that awful, bloody, tuneless voice of his.

'"Who beat the Wallabies?" he hollered. Flat as a pancake. "Who beat the Wallabies?" he repeated. Causin' a group of old men in the saloon bar to turn off their hearin' aids. "Who-ooo beat the Wallabies?" he screeched like a doctored owl, shatterin' several glasses behind the bar. "But good old Sospan Fach."

'Arms outstretched to what he saw as his adorin' public, he stood for a moment, drunkenly grinnin' and wavin' as he waited for the applause. Then he had a go at a deep bow, fell ass over tip off the chair and lay hiccupin' on the floor until three of us carried him off to the door.

'Outside, laughin' like a drain, he knocked over the sign advertisin' the pub's home cooked meals, slipped flat on his face gettin' up the bus steps, collapsed into his seat, demanded another Guinness, gave me an inane grin and fell sound asleep.

'By a unanimous decision at a special meetin' of the selection committee held on the bus on the way to Swandiff, the captain was dropped for that afternoon's game.

'The rugby posts stood in a rough field full of cows'.

'We arrived at our destination at two-thirty for a three o'clock kick off. At first sight neither the village nor its rugby club seemed much to write home about. The rugby posts stood in a rough field full of cows, with a small hut in one corner, under some trees. Fifteen men in red and yellow striped jerseys and white shorts were tryin' hard to shoo the cows into the field next door.

'"Sorry about this lads. Gareth should 'ave done it this mornin'. Silly bugger forgot." The Swandiff skipper, breakin' away from his cowboy work, puffed over to welcome us.

'"No 'arm done though. You get changed. We'll

'ave 'em out of 'ere in no time." He pointed to the hut and puffed off.

'Apart from a few benches and some coat hooks on the walls, the hut was empty. Shiverin', those Wanderers selected to defend the honour of Mellstock that afternoon, reluctantly began to change into rugby gear.

'Leavin' them to it, I had a quick look at our sleepin' beauty on the bus, and then made a full inspection of the Swandiff facilities. It took me all of thirty seconds. In addition to the hut, there was a lean-to shed behind it, and behind that, by the hedge, a crude enclosure of sackin' and poles marked Gents.

'HQ in the local pub perhaps, I surmised. But I wasn't hopeful.

'On the pitch, the cows were gone, and the Swandiff cowboys, armed with large shovels, were busily tryin' to remove what they had left behind. At three o'clock precisely they downed tools and lined up for the kick-off.

'It was an interestin' game Rich. Both teams started slowly. The Wanderers because of the journey and the beer they'd put away. The Swandiff cowboys because of their recent labours with our four-footed friends.

'At half-time the score was nil-nil.

'In the second half each side seemed to get a second wind, but then towards the end, they both faded badly.

'Swandiff won. 18-10 I think it was. Because their second wind lasted longer than ours, so they faded later than we did.

'But it wasn't any of that that made the game interestin'. It was our sleepin' beauty in the bus. He woke up.

'About half way through the second half the spectators had been forced to make a strategic withdrawal of about ten yards from the touchline. The pong from the pitch of trampled cow-pats havin' become so nauseating as to turn even the strongest stomachs.

'It was a mistake. Anyway on the part of the Mellstock members of the small crowd. It gave Dai more room for manoeuvre when he made his break.

'We were about ten minutes from the end of the game and I had forgotten all about him. As far as I was concerned he was still sleepin' off his mornin' boozin'. But I was wrong. Not only had he come to, but he'd been at the Guinness yet again. Suddenly there he was, on the steps of the bus, a bottle of the Irish nectar in each hand, bawlin' out his favourite song.

'"Who-ooo beat the Wallabies?" He reprised. Miles off key, as usual. And at maximum volume. "Who-oooo beat the Wallabies? 'Twas good old Sospan Fach."

'That was bad enough Rich. But that wasn't all. Far from it. Not only was the silly sod, as drunk as a newt. He was also starkers. Absolutely bollock naked. Unless you count his pants. Which he was wearing on his head.

'As we all turned to stare, he posed for a moment, lookin' like a bizarre, nude, Welsh version of Yasser Arafat, only taller. Then he emptied one of his bottles.

Tossed it aside. And snatchin' the pants from his brow and swingin' them round his head like a stripper, took off for a trip up the touchline.

'The Swandiff ladies among us all cheered wildly.

'"Who beat the Wobblies?" he shouted in return. Wavin' the pants in the air. "Who-ooooooooo beat the Wobblies? But goo' ole postman Pat." He shrieked with laughter, hurled his pants aloft and caught them neatly on the neck of his second Guinness bottle.

'The Swandiff ladies cheered even louder than before. And wolf-whistled like mad. I and the non-playing Wanderers closed in.

'Before we could get to him, he legged it further up the touchline. There he stopped. And pinched his nose between finger and thumb.

'"Pooh," he bawled. "Quel Pong. Urgh. Urgh. Urgh." he grabbed his throat and wrapped his pants round his face like a gas mask.

'The Swandiff ladies loved it. They cheered, whistled and waved like teeny-boppers. Dai was delighted. He bowed low to them, flourishin' his pants like Sir Walter Raleigh offerin' his cloak to Good Queen Bess. Then he was off again just too quickly for us to get him.

'Somewhere near the corner flag, he paused, finished off his second Guinness. And launched the bottle in our direction.

'"Take that you buggers," he shrieked, "Serve you right for makin' this bloody awful pong. Filthy beasts." He doubled up laughin'.

'The bottle missed by yards.

'The Swandiff ladies fell about in ecstasy. And

cheered their hero to the echo.

'But our captain's time was up. He'd dallied just a bit too long.

'He made one last desperate break infield. Obviously wantin' to plant his pants between the posts for one, final, glorious try.

'But he'd forgotten about the cows.

'A misplaced foot. A slitherin' fall. And we had him.

'"Come in number ten' I said 'your time is up".

'Gingerly we grabbed him by any part that was clean and carried him, protestin', to the changin' hut. The Swandiff ladies booed us roundly every step of the way. At the other end of the pitch, a triple blast on the whistle told us the match was over.

'Inside the hut, things had been happenin'. A row of long, portable baths full of steamin' water had been introduced. Thankfully we dumped our burden straight into the nearest one and left him to soak. He was asleep again within two minutes.

'I fetched his clothes from the bus, gave him half an hour's snooze, and after we'd dried and dressed him, took him for a slow, soberin' stroll around the field. We walked at a snail's pace. Dai was sunk in the depths of boozer's gloom.

'In the far corner, by the hut, cars were now parked. We saw a farm lorry come and go several times.

'Dark brown tea and dry sandwiches, I thought. Served in a damp, smelly ablutions hut. Marvellous. Bloody marvellous.

'But when we finally got back, the hut was shut

up. And all the noise was comin' from behind it. We went to see what was goin' on.

'The two teams were congregated around a large bonfire. Chatterin' away like stink, and helpin' themselves to beer from barrels set up on a long trestle table. Spirits risin' rapidly, I mingled. Our esteemed skipper, still deep in gloom, slipped quietly away into the hut.

'An hour later, merry as a nest of crickets, we all joined him.

'Air fresheners, paraffin lamps, portable heaters, tables, chairs, snow white cloths, crockery, cutlery, and the Swandiff ladies, had transformed the place. We packed in and enjoyed one of the finest rugby suppers I've ever had in my life.

'The dark brown beer flowed sweet as a nut, Rich. The singin' was out of this world. And we had more toasts than a mayor's banquet. We raised our glasses to everybody and everythin' we could think of. To rugby. To Wales. To Swandiff. To England. To Mellstock. To the past and the future. To absent friends. To ourselves. But especially to the Swandiff ladies and their marvellous food.

'How they did it I'll never know. But they did. Women are wonderful creatures, Rich. Don't ever forget that.

'We had steaks bigger than our plates. Strings of great, burstin' sausages. Cold ham that melted in your mouth. Mountains of golden chips. And mounds of crusty apple pie smothered with thick, farmhouse cream. It was a schoolboy's dream. We loved it. Except for Dai of course, who spent the evenin' sittin' quietly in the corner, at a table with the ladies, strugglin' with a ham sandwich and a cup of weak tea.

'And when it was over, and we'd downed the last of the sweet brown beer' Rich, we picked our way across that pongy old field to the bus. Royally fed. Cheerfully drunk. And happy as sandboys, as we assured our hosts that never could any rugby tour, anywhere, at any time, have got off to a more splendid start.

'Our captain, who'd already slipped away to his seat, was dragged out again by popular request. The Swandiff ladies had a song for him they said. An old Welsh folk ditty.

'Dai stood on the bus steps blushin' and grinnin' as they all sang out, loud and clear in the crisp night air. We didn't understand a word of their Welsh. But obviously he did. I learned later that it was an ancient, Celtic version of that old American jazz standard "A good man is hard to find." Or is it vice versa perhaps?

'Anyway, we left to wild cheerin', shoutin' and wavin'. With Dai lookin' highly embarrassed and secretly delighted, as the Swandiff ladies to a woman, all pouted their mouths and blew him huge farewell kisses.

'He slept with a smug smile on his face all the way to our tour HQ – the Seahorse Hotel on Swansea Bay. And when we got there about ten, even agreed to join the rest of us for a nightcap.

'We made straight for the residents' bar. Ours by right since we'd booked every bedroom in the place.

'Except one, apparently.

'For as we crowded in, someone was already there.

'Standin' at the bar counter, neat as ninepence, tankard in hand, moustache quiverin' with a welcomin' smile that split his face, was the man from Pontyberem himself – Mr Ivor Roberts.

'"Noswaith da," he said, "Bass or Worthington?" '

Chapter 8

The Gypsy's Curse

'Half three,' said Uncle R. 'I'll make us a cup of tea.'

He heaved himself out of his deck-chair, threw his Panama on to the footstool, gathered up the enamel jug and beer glasses, and stumped off into the pavilion.

In the still warm October sun, I drifted off into a doze.

He woke me up dumping the tray on the grass and collapsing into his seat.

'Best comedian the club ever had – old Windy Wagstaff,' he announced, apropos of bugger all. 'Tall chap, big shoulders, red, white and blue tie, played on the wing. Bloody marvellous "Champion Spitter of Gweat Bwitain." Even better "Gypsy's Curse." '

He laughed out loud at the thought.

I stretched lazily, yawning as I turned to face him.

'Keepin' you up are we?' he enquired.

'Sorry, Unk. Rude of me. No reflection on your Swandiff story though. Bloody funny that was. Old Dai was obviously quite a card. And I wouldn't have minded meeting those Swandiff ladies myself. Lovely grub, eh? Literally. But what's all this crap about Windy Wagstaff, the Champion Spitter, and some blooming gypsy? Who did they play for?'

He gazed at me pityingly.

'Oh, Rich,' he said. 'I love you dearly. You are without doubt my absolute favourite nephew...'

'You've only got one, Unk,' I intervened.

He ignored me.

'...but you really are an ignorant little sod when it comes to rugby. Do you seriously expect me to believe that you – a dedicated player and lover of God's own game for getting on for ten years now – have never heard of the Spitter and the Curse?'

'Yes, I am,' I said. 'No. I mean. Yes I do. I mean I haven't. Heard of them, that is. Oh hell. You know what I mean, Unk. Anyway, who are they?'

He sighed, sucked his teeth, and handed me a dirty mug of dark, brown tea, and a squashed bit of Swiss roll.

'Not who. What.' he growled. 'Monologues, Rich. Monologues. Windy was the best monologuer, monologuian, monologuist – reciter – I've ever heard in my life. He was a bloody wonder. An absolute scream. And the one about the gypsy cursing the vicar's house with fartin' was his star turn. A real killer.'

He laughed out loud again.

'Thanks, Unk. Fascinating I'm sure. But tell me. Because I'm just the incy winciest bit confused. What the hell have the prize routines of some defunct old stand-up comic got to do with the 1960 Mellstock Wanderers' Welsh Tour?'

'You can be a sarcastic little toad when you feel like it, can't you?'

He gave me a withering look and cut himself a

ragged slice of the Swiss roll.

'The point is, you young floater, that the Gypsy's Curse came true on that tour. When we played Carport in the second match. On the Saturday afternoon.'

He snorted and shook his head.

'Youth of today. God help us. No bloody manners. No respect for their elders and betters. Could do with a boot up the backside if you ask me.'

He took a swig from his mug.

I smiled inwardly and took a sip from mine. The tea had a funny taste. A bit like liniment. I wondered idly whether Uncle R kept his back rub in the bar fridge with the milk.

'Sorry, Unk. No offence meant. And none taken, I hope. Thanks for the tea by the way. Interesting flavour. Tastes a bit like Lapsang Suchong.'

I gave him an enquiring look.

'Who does he play for?' he said, grinning.

'London Chinese, Unk.' I grinned back. 'Part of that all Beijing threequarter line. Along with Oo Flung Dung, Long Dong Silver and Chris P Noodles. But let's not waste any more time with them. I'm on tenterhooks here. Waiting to hear more about this Gypsy's Curse thing. And for you to tell me exactly what happened at Carport.'

He looked at me sideways, his turkey eyes narrow with suspicion. But I'd made him the offer he could never refuse. So he took another swig from his mug. Smacked his lips. And carried on.

'We should never have had those couple of pints before kick-off. That's where we cocked it, Rich. But temptation was put in our way. And we fell. The Carport HQ was in a pub, see. The Black Ram. The same pub that Dai and I had met Mr Roberts of Pontyberem in the year before. When we went to the Arms Park.

'The club used to play on the field next door when it was a real village. But that was a long time ago. They've been a suburb of Cardiff for donkey's years now. And their pitch is a couple of miles away in a council park. But they still change and shower at the Ram. And they've got their own private bar there as well. That's where the trouble started. The hospitality was very friendly. The beer wasn't.'

He sniffed, sucked down his tea and refilled his mug.

'None for me, Unk,' I said, 'Delicious, but one's enough.'

Again he gave me the sideways look. Cockerel eyes suspicious. But again he made no comment.

'That local bitter started to make itself felt when we were changin',' he went on. 'We had to do that in a skittle alley behind the bar. By which time we were all sufferin' from a pretty nasty attack of the bloats. But we couldn't let on. Nor, much to our disappointment, Rich, could we let off.'

He giggled.

'You see, we weren't the only ones there. Two local ladies' skittle teams were battlin' it out in some match or other. So we had to grit our teeth, batten the old hatches, and hold tight until we could get outside.

'On our way to the ground things were different. Having been assured by our opponents during the pre-match drinks that they had their own transport, we'd let our driver take the bus off into the middle of Cardiff for a couple of hours. The Carport vehicle that replaced him wasn't exactly what we'd expected.

'"We don't bother with hiring a bus," their skipper explained. "Our President lends us one of his vans."

'It turned out to be a furniture van. One of those huge pantechnicons. Size of a small house. But with no windows. "Move in peace with Amos Dawkins" it said on the side. "We go anywhere, anytime."

'So we did the same. We took old Amos at his word. All of us. Both teams; two touch judges; the referee, and a gaggle of supporters. Everyone who'd been at the pre-match party. We took Mr Dawkins at his word. We had to. We had no choice. We were in agony. It was either wind-down or a busted gut. Or anyway it felt like that.

'But as I said, the van had no windows. Talk about the Black Hole of Carport, Rich. Talk about sulphretted hydrogen in the chemmy lab. Somethin' nasty in the woodshed. Dead rat under the floorboards. Niffy, niffy, plus, plus, it was. And boy, were we glad when we finally arrived at the ground and they let us out into the fresh air!

'But what happened en route to the match was nothing compared to what happened durin' it. Merely the openin' salvoes, you might say, of what turned out to be a heavy – and if you'll excuse the expression, Rich – long-winded barrage.

'The Carport Number One Burton was only just startin' to fizz.'

Chapter 9

Playing With The Wind

'So what actually happened at the match Unk? You did play it, did you?'

Uncle R chuckled.

'Oh yes. We played it all right Rich. I'll never forget it as long as I live. It was a complete and utter shambles. Real Fred Karno stuff. Cruelty to dumb animals on the pitch. But bloody funny to watch. The local supporters on the touchline cheered us off the field at the end. Said it was the most enjoyable game they'd seen all season. And asked "Was it true that it was the final of the Gas Board Cup?"

'The Black Ram's beer dominated the proceedin's from start to finish. Makin' its presence felt right from the kick-off. With Dai Davies as it's first victim.

'Havin' spent ages tryin' to tee the ball up without actually bendin' down to do it, he then forgot himself, and tried his usual long kick to the Carport goal line. But this time it was just too much for him. He made the distance all right, but as he followed through with that elegant style of his, he inadvertently let such a fierce one go that it seemed to reverberate round the whole ground and threaten the roof of the flimsy Corporation stand.

'That did it for both teams, Rich. Crippled with

laughin', we all started to run to where the ball was landin'. In our inflated state, it was fatal. A volley rang round the pitch that the fusiliers would have been proud of. Players fell on each other's shoulders and collapsed in hysterical heaps all over the field. Spectators cheered. Birds scattered. Babies howled. Dogs bolted. A passing park-keeper accidentally stabbed himself in the toe with his rubbish stick. And the referee blew up and ordered a scrum for general but unspecified foul play.

'It was a serious error. As the two eights packed down and took the strain, the Carport tight-head prop lit the fuse by firin' off a beauty. Our hooker slid one up the spout, closed the breech and replied with an absolute Bristol banger. And then all hell was let loose. It was just like an explosion in the firework factory. As the scrum heaved and twisted, we lost all control. Backfires of every sort and size flashed in every direction.

'Screams of mirth and groans of complaint rent the air. And finally the whole steamin' mass collapsed in helpless confusion.

'The spectators were convulsed. The referee looked quite frightened. And not darin' to ask us to re-form, warned both captains about conduct unbecomin', consulted with his touch judges, and awarded the home side a free kick.

'Thereafter he refused point-blank to have any more set scrums. And littered the game with penalties and free-kicks which nobody wanted to take in case they split their shorts doing so.

'But although the run of play was reduced to a

crawl, more entertainment was to come.

'The term "threequarter movement" took on a whole new meaning that afternoon Rich. I've never seen anythin' quite like it. Shy centres desperately tryin' to run with tightly clenched buttocks. Couldn't-care-less wings rockettin' along the touchline, blowin' off like demented sperm whales.

'Fortunately, as the interval approached, the ref and the two touch judges were obviously in a bit of trouble themselves. For after a brief pause while they ostensibly synchronised their watches, our arbiter announced he was blowin' for half-time, makin' no allowance for stoppages, and needed to have an urgent consultation with his colleagues behind the stand.

'Both sides were beginning to run out of steam by then anyway. Although sadly, Rich, not out of gas. And welcomed what turned out to be a considerably extended intermission.

'But despite spendin' the greater part of it lyin' face down on the turf and hopin' for relief – none came. The beer still bubbled in our guts like heavy water coming to the boil.

'As a result, the second half was, if anythin', worse than the first. Distension was rife. Flatulence abounded. And no matter which way we ran, force five winds were always at our backs.

'Thankfully, by this time, the referee, despite his sojourn behind the stand at half-time, was clearly suffering even more than we were. He stuck it for half an hour. Then, obviously *in extremis*, suddenly blew for full-time, declared the match a scoreless draw, and legged it for some nearby bushes convinced he would burst unless he could somehow manage the big one.

'Stragglin' into the furniture van, the rest of us volleyed and thundered our weary way back to the Black Ram and collapsed exhausted into the skittle alley. The local ladies' match was over by this time, so we were able to rest there in windy peace for the best part of an hour.

'That interlude, plus a supply of drinks produced by our hosts-peppermint, bicarbonate of soda, or angostura bitters-or all three together-finally put us right. The wind dropped. Our guts calmed down. And after a leisurely shower, we were ready for action again.

'It wasn't long in comin'.

'While we had rested, deflated and performed our ablutions, the Carport President had volunteered to put his guts on the line, and make a scientific tasting of all the beer they had available.

'Mr Amos Dawkins, brave man, drank off a crafty half from every one of the fourteen barrels in stock. And shortly before he passed out, declared every one of them to be completely free of the deadly, shirt-liftin' bug that had infected our lunchtime boozin'.

'To cheers all round we made our way to the private bar. The lady skittlers were already there. They were, they said, stayin' for the party.

Chapter 10

An Evening in Uplands

'And what a party it turned out to be, Rich.'

Uncle R lay back in his chair and finished off the last of the Swiss roll. The early October sun was just beginning to lose some of its unexpected Indian summer warmth. But it would be an hour or so yet before we'd need to fold up our deckchairs and retreat into the pavilion.

'Yes. Quite a thrash.' The session we'd had at lunchtime was Ovaltine-time with the Brownies compared with what happened that evenin'.

'First we had a bangers and mash supper. Then a bit of a knees-up. Real sophisticated entertainment, Rich. Beer an' skittles. Singin' an' dancin'-with beer.

And of course, now and then, between beers, a touch of the old slap an' tickle. I loved it.

'The skittle ladies were marvellous. They sang their heads off. Danced our legs off. Out-drank us at Cardinal Puff. And beat us down to the buff in the strip skittles competition.

'They sat on our knees, ran electric Welsh fingers through our hair. And whispered sweet Welsh nothings in our ears. They crooned us unintelligible, romantic Welsh songs. And then took us outside to explain what they were all about.

'For a simple, old prop forward like me, Rich, mid-twenties but young and innocent for my age, and still not quite dry behind the whats-its, It was life with a capital L. And I could have gone on livin' it all night.

'But it was over and done with by eight-thirty. Not for the rest of 'em. Just for Dai and me. Mr Roberts of Pontyberem arrived to take us off to another party. In a place called Uplands. Somewhere in the suburbs of Swansea. A cousin of his was havin' some sort of booze-up there. And in a weak moment the previous evenin' at the Seahorse, we'd agreed to go with him.

'It was, as it turned out, not a wise decision.

'We got to our destination about half nine. It took but a moment to see that it was some kind of special occasion. Fiftieth birthday party. Silver weddin' anniversary. That sort of thin'.

'Everybody except Mr Roberts of Pontyberem and us, were in dinner jackets. A major domo type let us in. There were private caterers, and waiters in white shirts and black ties to serve the drinks.

'There had been a sit-down supper at seven-thirty, the major domo told us. But sadly we'd missed it.

'Our hosts, Mr and Mrs Roberts (Uplands) didn't appear overjoyed when they found that their Pontyberem cousin had brought two extra guests with him. Especially guests in scruffy sweaters, no ties, smelling of bangers and beer, and obviously half-cut.

'But they put a brave face on it.

'"Noswaith da," said Mr Roberts (Uplands). "Champagne?" And beckoned a waiter over. Then he dragged off Mr Roberts (Pontyberem) to meet relatives, and left Dai and me to it.

'We stayed there in the front hall for two solid hours, Rich. And apart from the wine waiter, not a solitary sausage came anywhere near us.

'Somewhere about midnight we got fed up with it and went and looked for something to eat. The kitchen was empty except for a corgi dog half asleep in his basket, and a tabby cat curled up on the window sill. They greeted us like old friends.

'"Mush be a larder," Dai said, hiccupin'.

'"Assolutely. Spod on," I agreed, grinnin' at the corgi.

'"Wuff, wuff," the dog announced excitedly. Trotted over to a door and began scratching on it knowingly.

'He was right. There was a larder. And in it, on the main shelf, right in front of our eyes, lay a large cooked turkey on a dish. It smelled delicious.

'Beckonin' the cat to join us, we crowded in and shut the door.

'"Jus' leave id to me," Dai announced with a drunken giggle. "I'll be mother." And he took the turkey lovin'ly into his arms. The cat purred loudly. The corgi's tail thumped approvin'ly on the floor.

'The captain and I had a drumstick each. Our animal friends were awarded wings. We all finished about the same time.

'"Seconds?" Dai enquired, grinnin' inanely.

'"Don't mind if I do," I said, grinnin' back.

'The cat purred deep in her throat and put a gentle claw in my leg. The corgi gave an excited growl.

'Generous portions of white meat and stuffing were passed round to all. And we began to eat again.

'But this time we didn't finish together. We didn't finish at all in fact. Someone had at last come to see us.

'The door flew open. In silent astonishment Mr and Mrs Roberts (Uplands) stood surveying the scene. Behind them Mr Roberts (Pontyberem) looked pensive. Mouths clamped on their portions, the cat and dog melted quietly away. Mrs Roberts (Uplands) spoke.

'"Please," she said icily, "put down that fowl, will you. It's for tomorrow's luncheon."

'Like naughty schoolboys we returned our gnawed turkey pieces to the dish.

'"Sorry pardon," Dai mumbled, shakin' his head, "Shouldna done id."

'"Yeah, ver' sorry," I added, "bud we were hungry."

'We brushed crumbs of stuffin' from our chins and tried to look contrite.

'Mr Roberts (Uplands) had a face like an open razor.

'Behind him, his cousin was doin' his best not to laugh.

'He looked at us. We looked at him. He did his damnedest to hide his amusement in a cough.

'But it was no good. His shoulders started to shake. And the first, half-choked sob came out.

'That did it. Before we could stop ourselves the three of us had dissolved into uncontrollable laughter.

'We shrieked, Rich. We howled. We wailed. Our eyes poured. We doubled up in helpless, hysterical agony. Slapping our thighs as we fought for breath.

'Through our tears, as we did our best to straighten up, we peered at our host and hostess. One look at their stony, tight-lipped faces and we were off again.

'We bellowed. We bawled. We moaned. We caught our breath. "Oh God," we spluttered. "Oh my God." "Oh my merry God." We could hardly stand for laughin'.

'"Argh... argh... argh... argh," we choked. Clingin' to the door for support. "Ooh... ooh... ooh" we screamed as we tried desperately not to fall down.

'We did our utmost to say we were sorry again. But we couldn't. We wanted to. But we just couldn't speak any more.

'In the end Mr and Mrs Roberts (Uplands) gave us up, led us to the car, and retired without a word, bangin' the front door behind them.

'Sadly the crash set us off again. And for several more minutes we rolled about in the car until our jaws ached from laughin'.

'When we drove away at last and headed for the Seahorse at Mumbles, we were still teeterin' on the edge of hysteria.

'Finally Mr Roberts recovered sufficiently to speak.

'"Silly bugg-ers," he declared. "Not you, them. All that fuss over a bit of bloody turkey. Sorry lads. My apologies. But let's get back to the hotel and have a pint of Worthin'ton. My shout."

'It was the longest speech I'd ever heard him make.

Chapter 11

The Great Leveller

We had turned our deckchairs so as to get the best of the late sun. Uncle R was in high good humour. Suddenly he broke into verse.

'It was an October evenin'
Old Ronnie's work was done,
And he before the pavilion door
Was sittin' in the sun.
And by him sleepin' like a clod
His nephew Richard, lazy sod.'
He cackled.

I ignored him and his mashed up version of Southey.

'I feel like a pint,' I said, stretching and stifling a yawn.

'I wish you were, Rich, I wish you were.'

He cackled again. Got out his tobacco pouch and started the ritual of filling his old bulldog briar.

'Get us a jug of beer and my tankard, will you, dear boy. And a glass for yourself of course.'

He put a match to the pipe and blew out a stream of perfumed Erinmore smoke.

'Then I'll tell you about the final match of that Easter Tour. The one we won.'

Ten minutes later he did just that.

By this time we again had the enamel jug of bitter on the grass between us. On our respective chests were balanced my pint glass and his two-pint tankard. And we lay at peace with the world. The warm evening air around us scented by the silver smoke from his pipe.

'Sunday at the Seahorse was a dead loss,' he began. 'As you might expect, Rich. Bearin' in mind the shenanigans that went on the night before.

'It must have been half-midnight when Dai, Mr Roberts and I got back to the hotel from Uplands. The Wanderers' coach from Carport pulled in about half an hour later. We were just finishin'a quiet good-night pint in the hotel bar. And thinkin' of turnin' in. But the lads had other ideas.

'Stewed to the gills though every one of them was, they still demanded more booze. And insisted we join 'em.

'The Seahorse landlord, as you can imagine, was especially pleased. He stood there behind the bar, laughin' with sciatica, as we kept him pullin' pints until four. Then he called time. On the grounds that he was on duty again at eight.

'Whether he was or not I've no idea, Rich. But if he was he was wastin' his time. There wasn't much of a call for breakfast on the Sunday mornin'. Or for lunch, for that matter. Most of the Wanderers surfaced about three. Feelin' like death. And ready to sign the pledge. The hotel's public rooms looked like a casualty clearin' station.

'Dai, Mr Roberts and I chose to clear our own thick heads by gettin' out and about, and keepin' busy.

We spent the day sittin' in a nearby bay watchin' the tide come in and start to go out again. That, plus a quiet dinner and an early night, brought us back to somethin' approachin' normality by breakfast time on Easter Monday.

'But we were in the minority. The Seahorse sittin' rooms that mornin' still looked more like a convalescent home than a hotel. And by midday we were still one short for the afternoon game against Newsea.

'It looked as though we'd had it. No alternative but to play with fourteen men. Or ask our opponents to lend us a player. But then Dai came up with the answer. He drafted Mr Roberts into our side. It was obvious. It was also a master stroke.'

Uncle R paused. Ostensibly for refreshment. But also, I suspect, for dramatic effect. He removed his tankard from his chest. Raised himself up. Refreshed his drink. Swigged half of it off in one go. And resumed his tale.

'The man from Pontyberem may have been at least fifteen years older than the rest of us Rich. But he turned out to be a prop in a thousand. A real pit prop of a prop, in fact.

'He scrummaged like a bull in a pen. His opposite number must have felt that he was shovin' against a pillar box. Or tryin' to hold back a chargin' rhino. And woe betide you if he caught you in the loose. It felt – as one Newsea forward whom he had tackled from behind testified later – as if the good old rock of ages had landed smack in the small of your back.

'It wasn't so much that he strengthened our side,

Rich. More that he inspired it. Seein' him, nearly old enough to be the father of most of our players, chargin' round the field like a two-year old, dispensin' mayhem in all directions, cheered us up so much, we felt we daren't let him down by losin'.

'So we didn't.'

'Newsea is a minin' village and we kicked off on a pitch sliced out of the side of a small, green, daffodil-covered mountain that had obviously once been a slag heap. The playin' surface was rock hard, flat as a pancake, and more black than green. When you were tackled on it, you got up slowly and tended to limp for a while. As well as lookin' like a coalman.

'The home side reckoned it was worth ten points to them.

'We didn't doubt it. And that, coupled with the general cragginess of their pack, who looked as if they'd been hewn rather than born, would normally have instilled in the Wanderers an instant inferiority complex.

'Bearin' in mind our previous record, Rich, we would probably have accepted, ten minutes after kick-off, that if defeat wasn't already starin' us in the face, then it was givin' us a pretty old-fashioned look.

'Mr Roberts changed all that.

'We learned later that he had spent quite a few years in the minin' trade himself. And had played on more pitches like the Newsea one than we'd had hot dinners. We also learned that his nickname in the rugby world around Pontyberem was "the great leveller." Because his bone-shakin' tacklin' could take the steam out of the most high pressure opponents.

An ability that he proceeded, from the word go, to demonstrate to the Newsea miners.

'Within half an hour of the start we could definitely feel the benefit of his slowin' down process. The steel-plated Newsea pack was certainly beginnin' to buckle a bit. And during the half-time interval you could pick out the forwards he'd tackled more than once. They were lyin' down.

'By the end of the game, "the leveller" himself had slowed down to a walk. But by then he'd knocked so many rivets out of the opposin' iron men, that we were shovin' their scrum all over the place.

'We won by ten clear points. And in the pit-head baths where we sluiced down after the match, the Newsea miners gave Mr Roberts his due.

'"Typically bloody English," their skipper bawled through the steam, "beatin' us by playin' a bloody Welshman in your side. Crafty bastards."

'"Two," Dai bawled back, 'My Da was born in Splot.'

'"Better there than England I suppose," the Newsea skipper announced and left it at that.

'Mr Roberts of Pontyberem said nothin'. Even in the saloon bar of the Llewellyn Arms a little later, when he was toasted as "man of the match" by both sides, and called upon for a speech, he could only raise a few words in reply.

'Chumpin' his chops, clearin' his throat, and brushin' what seemed to be a speck of grit from his eye, he forced his way to the bar. "Thanks lads," he said. "Much appreciated. Pints all round."

'Moved by his generosity a Newsea miner

brought out his ukelele and struck up "Why was he born so beautiful." We settled down to the best sing-song of our Welsh visit.

'We sang of land and sea: the Ash Grove and the Good Ship Venus. We remembered famous men: the Minstrel Boy, the One-Eyed Reilly, Dan, Dan, The Lavatory Man, and Cousin Rupert who played outside-half for Newport. We demanded that Thora should speak, Poor Blind Nell see the mornin' sun, and Honey have a sniff on us. We dreamed of White Christmases, Cats on the roof-tops, Marble Halls and Miners' Homes.

"The log was burnin' brightly,
Twas a night that would banish all sin,
For the bells were ringin' the old year out
And the New Year in."

'The words thundered along the village street as we congregated round the bus in the pub car-park. Everybody shook hands with everybody else. The Newsea skipper made a brief farewell speech. Dai replied. Half as long. Twice as sentimental.

'Mr Roberts, since he was leavin' us as well as them, was forced to suffer the warm goodbyes of both teams.

'This caused him to get so much grit in his eye, he couldn't speak at all. He grasped Dai and me in turn in silent bear hugs, and nodded his head violently in thanks to all present.

'We filed into the bus still singin'.
"We'll see you again,
Whenever Spring breaks through again."
'We stood, wavin' from the windows.

'"Cheerio Newsea. God Bless," we bawled. "We got style. We got class. We got the team to tan your ass."

'There was a great shout from our opponents. The whole village seemed to be gathered there in the moonlight. Then, led by the man with the ukelele, and with Mr Roberts wavin' madly at the front, they started on their farewell song:

"We'll keep a welcome in the hillsides,' they sang.
We'll keep a welcome in the vales,
This land of ours will keep a welcome
Till you come back again to Wales."

'The bus moved away, en route for Mellstock.

'Their singin' rolled after us. Down the village street and beyond. Along the road to England. Until finally it was lost in the darkness and the distance.

'It was a touchin' moment, Rich. Even our gang of half-slewed, self-centred, heathen young buggers were affected, as they settled down to sleep. A damp eye here and there. A bit of snivellin'. And especially from old Dai of course. He snuffled away next to me for at least ten minutes. Partly boozer's gloom, I suspect. But touchin' none the less.

'And then, on the Saturday after we got back, we had the celebration of our famous victory. Everybody happily sloshed. Glasses raised to the tourin' side who'd broken the Wanderers' duck. And a unanimous decision taken to order for all prepared to stump up a fiver, a suitably engraved, two-pint, commemorative tankard. Mr Roberts of Pontyberem, of course to be sent one gratis.

Uncle R flourished his own tankard in my

direction, drained it, and reached for the jug. It was empty. The sun was slipping towards the horizon. The air was getting chilly. He got to his feet and folded his deckchair. He too seemed to be having a little trouble with grit in the eye.

I folded my chair in turn and followed him into the pavilion. He stowed the chairs away, and drew us two pints from the bar.

Then, gazin' into the middle distance, he said quietly, 'I know you think I'm a sentimental old fool, Rich. But it really was a bloody good tour. And despite what you said earlier about you and your mates, I reckon they might well have liked it.'

'I reckon so too, Unk,' I said, gently gripping his shoulder. 'I know I would have. So how about a toast?'

He looked surprised.

'Toast? Who to?'

I smiled.

'To whom, Unk, surely. To whom?'

He had the grace to laugh.

'Ok, Rich. Touché. To whom then? The Queen. The RFU? You and those mates of yours?'

'Wrong, Unk. None of them. To The Wanderers. To old Dai. To Mr Roberts of Pontyberem. To Swandiff, Carport and Newsea. To the 1960 Tour of South Wales. And last, but by no means least, to the best teller of rugby tales I know. You, you old bastard.'

Chapter 12

Rhondda Valli

It was one of those days that sort out the rugby men from the boys. As I walked across the Mellstock pitch, a Siberian wind blew bullets of rain into my chest that stopped my breath.

I'd come to the ground a couple of hours early because I'd had a hard morning and needed a stint by the bar fire with my feet up before I had to change for the game.

Apart from the groundsman in his cubby hole oiling his equipment, and two young wives making sandwiches in the kitchen, the pavilion was empty. Except for the bar where someone was doing a Garbo in an ancient armchair by the fire. It was a Mellstock tradition that in cold weather we always lit an old-fashioned, open, coal fire in the bar on match days.

The old devil's asleep, I thought, as I crept up behind him. But he wasn't. Uncle R sat with elbows on his knees, gazing vacantly into the red coals.

'Ronnie Valli's gone,' he said mournfully when he saw who the intruder was. 'I heard this mornin'.'

I dumped my bag and pulled up a chair beside him.

'Gone, Unk? What d'you mean, gone?'

'Gone. Finished. Kaput.' He was obviously not in

the best of moods. 'What's the matter with you, Rich? He's done for. Departed. Passed over. Popped his clogs. Kicked the bucket. You know. Dead.'

He sniffed and turned back to the fire. I pulled a rude face at the back of his head.

'Sorry, Unk, I'm sure. Pardon me for existing. But who the hell was Ronnie Valley? Some antique pop star? Son of Rudy Vallee perhaps?' My father had a collection of old American dance band records, including some by a chap called Rudy Vallee and his Connecticut Yankees. I was tickled pink I'd remembered the name.

Uncle R wasn't.

'Saucy little bugger, you are, young Rich. No sympathy. And pig ignorant with it. Ronnie Valli was a respected member of this club for donkey's years.'

'Not in my time he wasn't.'

'So he was before your time. So what. There was life in the Mellstock RFC before 1994 you know. Or whenever it was you joined the club. It didn't all start the day you kindly decided to grace us with your scintillatin' company.'

He breathed a heavy sigh. And I could almost hear his mind turning over. 'Youth of today. Bloody hopeless. Selfish little buggers. Need a good toe up the jaxi.'

I opened my mouth to protest. But thought 'No. He's had bad news. Poor old sod's upset. Not the right moment to start taking umbrage.' So I didn't. Especially as I was just beginning to get warm by the fire.

'OK, Unk. Keep your hair on. I'm sorry you've

lost an old friend. I really am. But you've gotta realise I've absolutely no idea whom – note the "whom" Unk – you're talking about. Who was this Ronnie Valley character anyway?'

I waited. He was silent for a moment. Then he turned back to me. He had the grace to look contrite.

'Beg pardon, Rich. I'm feelin' a bit off-side this mornin'. As I'm sure you've noticed. News came as a bit of a shock, to be honest. Though I dunno why. I haven't thought about old Ronnie for years. And I would have sworn he hadn't thought much about me either. Until today.

'Either way, I shouldn't have taken it out on you. Bloody stupid of me. Because, come to think of it, you couldn't possibly have known Ronnie Valli. How could you? It must be fifteen years ago or more that he left Mellstock. When you were only a kid. And he would've been in his sixties then. Still, it's sad to think the old bugger's no longer with us.'

He shook his head.

'We called him Ronnie, but his real name was Owen Llewhellin Vittorio Valli. VALLI, by the way, not VALLEY. His father migrated from Italy to Pontypridd of all places. Married a Welsh girl. And opened up his barber shop. Ronnie followed in his father's footsteps. Learned the trade in dad's emporium. And then moved on. First to Oxford. And then to Cambridge. Before comin' here and settin' up in business for himself.

'Apparently the Latin Quarter of Cowley and the old Polytechnic of the Fens had fascinated him since childhood. So as soon as he was 17 he left home and visited them both. One after the other. And spent fifteen years in each. One of the best scissors and comb men Oxbridge ever produced, so I'm told.

'It must have been the late sixties when he arrived in Mellstock. He turned up in the bar here one day. Large as life. Welsh as laver bread. And introduced himself. 'I'm an Iti barber from the Welsh valleys, amicos. And proud of it.' he announced. 'Call me Rhondda. Everybody does. And barman – drinks all round.'

'So we did as he asked, Rich. Drank his health. And called him Rhondda. Except that within a week we'd all shortened it to Ronnie.'

'Close buddy of yours, was he, Unk?'

Uncle R sucked his teeth.

'Wouldn't say that. I liked him all right. But to be honest it was more a case of him liking me. And all because I took him a "get-well-soon" card when he was in hospital.'

'Nice of you,' I said.

'Case of havin' to really,' he went on. 'You know me, Rich, when it comes to friends in need. Most of the time I reckon they're a bloody nuisance. But when he went in to have his guts repaired, someone had to take him the standard club card and bunch of grapes. And with my Infirmary connection through your dad, I naturally enough clicked for the job. Even though, up to then, I'd never been a particular buddy of his. He, of course, bein' considerably older than me.'

He sat back in his chair and gave me a warning look. I smiled sweetly and swallowed the 'He sixty. You fifty-nine,' comment I'd had in mind.

'Tell me more,' I said, stretching myself out and putting my feet on the fender.

'Well, when I called in to see him, he was not in the best of moods. He'd been in the ward for several days. Havin' some sort of preliminary tests that involved him bein' kept in a side-room all on his own. Which for a barber, of course, amounted to acute mental cruelty. Time on his hands and not a sausage to talk to.

'And that wasn't all. There was worse. He'd been sworn off the booze as well. Which for a dedicated Worthington E man like him, really was the fate worse than death. The kick in the goolies to a poor bloke who was already down.

'He accepted the soggy bag of grapes without comment. And read the card without the glimmer of a smile.

'"Get well soon" it said 'Convalescence already arranged for you in a Truss House at Hernia Bay. Hope you have a rupturous time. Best wishes from all your fellow supporters of the oval ball."

'As rugby wit goes, we thought it rather good. But he was in no mood for humour.

'Rampant with self-pity, all he wanted to do was tell someone – anyone – how badly the hospital was treatin' him.

'"That bible-punchin' little sod, Dr Bumfart" he announced bitterly, "and that temperance bitch Wendy Fatass. They've stuck me in this side-room all on my tod. And then point-blank refused to let me have a drink. Just my luck. My first time ever in hospital, and I click for a quack with religious mania, and a teetotal bloody nurse sufferin' from chronic ingrowin' virginity."

'I gathered from a little polite questioning that Dr Brumfit, the house surgeon, was Chairman of the Infirmary's Young Christians' Association. And that Ward Sister Wendy Brodsterne, was a well-known local white ribboner.

'"Bugger me," he moaned, "it's bad enough knowin' that some cack-handed old surgeon is gonna stick a knife in your guts tomorrow, without havin' loonies like Bumfart and Fatass to put up with as well. God, I'd give my right arm for a Worthie."

'"Nil Desperandum," I said. Raisin' my right hand like a bishop givin' a blessin'. "Don't panic. Hold on to your arm. And I'll see what I can do."

'I meant well, Rich. I meant it as a bit of a joke. But he didn't take it that way. And I can see now why. He didn't know me. And to him I must have sounded a real pompous twat.

'"You?" he said. Lookin' at me as if I was some kind of bed bug. Partly surprised, partly irritated and highly sceptical.

'I bridled slightly. "Yes, me, I said."

'"How come?" His surprise and irritation were wanin' a bit. His scepticism wasn't.

'"I happen to know a few people here," I said airily. "May be able to pull the odd string or two."

'"Really?" He was still doubtful. But interested. "Who d'you know?"

'"Well, my brother you see. He's the Infimary Secretary."

'"Hmm," he said. There was a pathetic flicker of

hope in his eyes.

'"Trust me," I said. "Thousands wouldn't. But trust me. I promise I'll do my best."

'He almost smiled. "Get on then," he said. "And God bless your little cotton socks."

'"It didn't take much to work the oracle, Rich. The chap he called the cack-handed surgeon had played a couple of seasons in the second row for Mellstock in his day. And was highly sympathetic to Ronnie's problem. He gave the appropriate instructions to the evangelical Dr Brumfit, and, much to the houseman's and Wendy Ward Sister's disgust, Ronnie found himself written up on the drug sheet for two pints of ale a day on medical grounds for the length of his stay.

'For a six pints a day man it wasn't a lot. But it was Worthington. And it was free. And he never forgot it.

'"You saved my life," he told me some weeks later when he was fully recovered and back in circulation. "And Ronnie Valli never forgets a good turn."

'He was pullin' on his jersey next to me at the time. Ready to go on duty with the first side. Somethin' he'd done every week without fail, year in, year out, for close on a dozen seasons. Until his rupture forced him into the hands of the quacks.

'He was the best touch-judge the club's ever had. There was no doubt about that. Everyone said so. Includin' all our regular opponents. Everybody admired him. Everybody liked him. And everybody who'd ever had a few beers with him after the game was only too well aware of his little problem.

'It wasn't anythin' awful. And it wasn't at all uncommon. But he had it in a rather unusual way.

'He was a barber, remember. So of course he did rabbit on a bit. And he was gettin' on in years. So he was inclined to live in the past.'

Uncle R paused, raised his finger at me, and gave me a warning look.

'Rich,' he said, 'no sarky remarks now. OK?'

'Not a word, Unk,' I said, grinning. 'Not a word.'

'Anyway Ronnie's trouble was that, given a couple of drinks after a rugby match, there was no way he could stop himself from launchin' into long-winded stories about all the famous old players he'd met in the twenties, thirties and forties, durin' his barberin' days in Oxford and Cambridge.

'What he had to say was actually quite interestin'. But not to the vast majority of the denizens of the Mellstock RFC bar. Who didn't know any of these ancient rugby blokes he ponced on about from Adam. And who couldn't care less about them anyway. Which is why, for most of Ronnie's time at the club, whenever he started out on one of his ramblin' reminiscences, nobody really listened to him.

'Until, that is, he and I became all palsy-walsy as a result of my visit to him in the Infirmary.

'Once he came out of hospital, I only had to set foot in this bar, and he would insist on buying me a drink. And every time he bought me a drink, he would insist on tellin' me how grateful he was. "Ronnie Valli never forgets a good turn," he would say. "You saw me right in my hour of need, Ronnie.

And now I'm returnin' the compliment." And after he'd returned the compliment a couple of times, there was no escapin'. His obsession took over. And I had to hear the inside story of one of the Golden Oldies from his Varsity days.

'Indeed Rich, we became bar companions so often, everybody started callin' us The Two Ronnies. And in Ronnie's eyes, although not necessarily in mine, I became one of his best cronies.

"'Only bugger here,' he used to say, 'who's got the faintest damn interest in the game's history. Only bloody man in the whole club who's got an ounce of rugby romance in his bleeding soul. Only man really worth talkin' to."

'And the funny thing was, Rich, that while the rest of the lads were grinnin' behind their hands and givin' me their condolences, I was findin' Ronnie's tales more and more interestin'.

'That marvellous 1930s England wing, Prince Alex 'Obo' Obolensky, for example. Never bein' charged a penny by Ronnie's boss – a dyed in the wool royalist – for anythin' they did for him in the salon. And all because, on his very first visit, he'd come in with four friends, and the shop found itself holdin' a full-house of royalty. Princes over Kings. One in every chair.

'Then there were Obo's team-mates, 'Tuppy' Owen Smith and Tommy Kemp. Full-back and stand-off half. Who made him shave his head bald when he lost a bet with them on the result of the 1937 England-Wales match.

'Or Windsor Lewis and Cliff Jones. Two of

Wales' most brilliant out-halves of the late twenties. Arguin' with him in turn, every time they came in over several years, about who was Wales's best stand-off ever.

'And, an absolute favourite character, Welsh super centre, Wilf Wooller. Reckoned by some to be one of the best players in that position ever to appear in the Varsity Match. He visited Ronnie regularly, and swore by his "Freezers" – scalp massages with menthol – as the best hangover cures on the market. "Ronnie" he used to say, "for a bob, you do for me what my doctor couldn't do for five guineas."

'And those are just a drop in the bucket, Rich. There were literallly dozens more. As slowly but inevitably, I became his regular, weekly, captive audience of one.

'But not for all that long.

'Six months after he came back from the Truss House in Hernia Bay, he started makin' vague comments about leavin' Mellstock. And six months after that, he did.

'Some old barber colleague in the Fens Poly, who was gettin' a bit long in the tooth, wrote and suggested a partnership in a flourishin' shop that was becomin' too much for him to run on his own. And Ronnie accepted his offer.

'Just before he left to become the Vidal Sassoon of the Eastern Counties, the club gave him a grand goin'-away party. Which he insisted on attendin' in full touch judge regalia. Tweed cap, Mellstock jersey, flannel trousers, Mellstock socks, rugby boots and a club touch flag.

'He had a wonderful time. Pissed as a fart on Worthington E by nine-thirty, he had to be forced to hand over the club's touch flag, so that the Chairman could give him a special, de luxe, pure silk one with tassels and his name on it, as a leavin' present.

'And regularly throughout the evenin' he insisted on shakin' my hand, standin' me a drink, and announcin' with the sort of tear-jerkin' sincerity that only a drunken bum can muster, "Ronnie Valli never forgetsh a goo' turn."

'And that was the last time I saw him, Rich. He was gone within a week. And as far as I know, no-one in Mellstock ever heard from him again. Until this mornin'.'

Uncle R paused in his monologue, pulled himself up from his chair, and vanished through the little side door that gave access to the back of the bar.

'Need a drop of throat oil. Bit of a stiffener.' His voice came muffled through the shutters. 'Don't suppose you want anythin', as you're playin'.'

'No thanks, Unk. I gotta be on the field in three-quarters of an hour.'

I threw a couple of shovelfulls of coal on the fire. Uncle R reappeared, his face buried in his special two-pint tankard. He sat down, put his beer on the fender, and heaved a long sigh.

'Wasn't just a letter, you know,' he said 'There was a parcel too.'

'Parcel? What sort of parcel?'

'Thing done up in brown paper, you silly sod. What d'you mean – what sort of parcel?'

'I meant big or small, Unk. Long and thin. Or

short and fat. But let it pass. Anyway, who was the letter from?'

'His daughter of course. She said he'd died about a month ago, and she'd found this parcel in his wardrobe when she was goin' through his things. It was already addressed. And it had a note with it sayin' she should send it on to me after his death.'

'What was it, Unk? His special touch flag?'

'No. Nothin' like that. You'd never guess in a hundred years, Rich. So don't try. I'll tell you. It was a lot of programmes.'

'Programmes? What sort of programmes?'

'Varsity Rugby Match programmes. More than seventy of 'em. An unbroken collection. Startin' from the first time the match was played at Twickenham. 1922, I think it was. And comin' right up to last year. All in mint condition. From the thin, folded, pale blue, four-sided, cards they had in the twenties. "Official Programme – Threepence." To the plush, three quid, seventy-five page productions they have these days.

'Bloody marvellous, Rich. Real collector's item. And what's more important, packed of course, with the names of all Ronnie's old friends, from what he liked to call the Golden Age.'

He took a drink from his tankard, wiped his mouth with the back of his hand, and gazed contemplatively into the fire. When he turned back to me again his eyes were misty.

'Silly old sod,' he said, 'What did he want to go and do that for? After all these years? He didn't owe me anythin'. I owed him, more like. All those pints he bought me. Can't understand it.'

'I can, Unk. He liked you. And as he said, you probably are the only bloody man in the whole club who's got an ounce of rugby romance in his bleedin' soul. So who better to have his cherished programmes than you? I'm only surprised he didn't enclose a farewell note. Somethin' sayin' Ronnie Valli never forgets a good turn. That sort of thing.'

Uncle R was scathing.

'Don't be bloody silly, Rich. Ronnie may have had Italian blood in him, but at heart he was as British as you or me. He didn't hold with that sort of sentimental crap. Didn't go in for the emotional bit. Any more than I do. Anyway he didn't need to send a note. He knew I'd understand.'

He drank more beer. To hide my grinning face, I leaned forward and gave the fire a vicious poking.

After a brief silence he spoke again.

'Sometimes, Rich, I do wish I had a bit more sentimentality in me. Was a bit more like old Dai Davies who took me to the Arms Park all those years ago. I think he really did believe there was a sportin' Valhalla, up there above the clouds. A sort of Elysian fields where all Welsh rugby heroes went when they'd finished with life in the Principality.

'It would be nice to think so, wouldn't it? Nice to believe that old rugby players never die. They just get an eternal debenture seat in the big Twickers in the sky. It's a marvellous thought. Even though it's a load of old cobblers.'

He gave a short, derisive snort, and took yet another long pull from his tankard.

'But I must say it would be really good to think of old Ronnie now. Up there in Never Never Land. Perfect pitches. Perfect weather. Permanent September. Runnin' the line in a never-endin' series of Varsity Matches. Shadowin' Prince Obolensky to the corner flag for a try. Gaspin' at Wilf Wooller's pace and swerve, dummy and hand-off. Applaudin' Cliff Jones's jink and Windsor Lewis's outside break. And marvellin' at Tuppy Owen-Smith – the complete fullback.

'God it would be great stuff, wouldn't it, Rich? Somethin' to dream about on cold winter nights.'

'Certainly would, Unk. I only wish I could see it.'

I smiled at him affectionately.

But he didn't hear me. He was staring into the fire. Still wallowing in his sentimental fantasy.

'And he could be in all the team photos too. With both teams. And he could shake hands with all the VIPs – old Rugby Union Presidents, visitin' notabilities, Prince of Wales, King George V or VI even.'

He chuckled like a schoolboy.

'And best of all, Rich, when they're back in the pavilion after the games, Ronnie can buy them all beer. Standin' his round with the rest. "Same again Obo, Cliff, Wilf, Windsor, Tuppy, Tommy?" As he orders up the ambrosial Worthington E.

'And they'll stand there, Rich. Pints cradled in the crooks of their arms. As they laugh, swap jokes and reminisce. Just like all old rugby friends always do when they get together.'

He was misty-eyed again. Faint smile on his face.

Staring blankly into the middle distance.

He's going over the top, I thought. Please God don't let him start blubbing.

But I should have known Uncle R better.

He suddenly came to, turned to me and raised his glass.

'Shame those Elysian fields are a load of bullshine,' he said, with a rueful grin. 'Anyway, here's to you, Ronnie, you old bugger. Wherever you are. Iechyd da. And thanks for the programmes. Much appreciated, old friend.'

Don't tell him. But as I joined in the toast, my eyes were a bit misty too.

Chapter 13

Rugby Studs

The Grantley game always drew a good crowd. At least thirty. Largely Mellstock Golden Oldies. Still fuming. After fifty years. That a gang of renegade Mellstockians should have had the gall in 1949, to set up a rival club in the town. Just because they couldn't get a game in the Mellstock first side.

So every year, come the third Saturday in January, when Grantley were our visitors, the club's bus-pass brigade would screw on their wooden legs, get out their Zimmers, and stump down to the Mellstock ground crying for revenge. While Uncle R, who loved this fixture above all others – old cronies, hours of non-stop boozing and reminiscence, and a rugby match thrown in for good measure – spent most of the previous week preparing himself and the pavilion for the occasion.

This year, on the Thursday evening before the game, I decided to drop into the Mellstock ground on my way home, to see how he was getting on. Somewhat to my surprise, he had a visitor already. A man knocking on sixty. A solid-looking customer in a neat, albeit shabby, business suit. The two of them were enjoying a drink together at the bar and laughing like drains.

'Hey, Rich.' Uncle R beckoned me over to join them. 'Come and meet Anty. Good friend of mine. And one of Mellstock's really golden oldies. ANT Youngman. Welsh Trialist, Newport and Mellstock. Look him up in the records. One of the best outside halves never to have played for Wales. Silly sod.'

'Flatterer. You're only saying that because it's true. Apart from the silly sod bit.' Anty grinned. We shook hands.

The stranger's shirt was immaculate white. But sloppily ironed. His tie blue with white spots. Expensive silk. But slightly soiled at the knot. The blue silk handkerchief which decorated his breast pocket was just beginning to fray at the corners.

But his hands were scrubbed clean like a surgeon's. He wore a large gold signet ring, and his wrist-watch had a heavy gold bracelet. Under his shirt, I was sure, an equally heavy gold medallion nestled against a dark, hairy chest. Tanned by a foreign sun to a light coffee colour, his skin had a sort of bloom on it. As though dusted with talcum powder, that had also drifted in white streaks into his dark hair. His face was round like a baby's, with baby blue eyes that still retained something of their original innocence.

Slightly down at heel? Maybe. But an obvious ladies man. Right down to the tips of his polished finger nails.

Uncle R was in his working clothes. Old corduroys, trainers, Mellstock jersey and tattered fair-isle sweater. He'd been seeing to the beer in the bar store and was reviewing the fruits of his labours. He held up to the light the straight pint testing-glass of bitter he'd drawn off from the new barrel. And launched into the mantra that he kept specially for this situation.

'Clear as a virgin's pee. Pure as a maiden's prayer'.

'Look at that. A sight for sore eyes if I ever saw one. Clear as a virgin's pee. Pure as a maiden's prayer. A pint in a million. A really beautiful pint. Amber nectar at its best. Perfection in a glass. Beer as it ought to be. Good health.' He knocked off half of it in one swallow. Smacked his fleshy lips. And exhaled a long, appreciative "Aaaaagh."

'Thank the Lord for the Bible,' he announced. 'And heaps of other things.'

Anty was drinking whisky.

'Iechyd da,' he said.

My uncle turned to me.

'Haven't seen this old bugger for ages. Donkey's years. And now, fresh from a month in the bleedin' Caribbean, he just turns up here out of the blue. Like a bloody bad penny. God knows what he's been up to all this time. Says he's been runnin' a hotel in Peterborough. I should cocoa. Knockin' shop more likely. Knowin' him.'

He grinned at his visitor.

Anty raised his glass in reply.

'I love you too,' he said.

Uncle R sniffed.

'You might not think so to look at him now, Rich. But he wasn't a bad player in his day. Came off the same assembly line as Cliff Morgan, Barry John and Phil Bennett. The one old Max Boyce used to sing about. The special factory Wales had for turnin' out top quality outside halves. Like my old pal Dai Davies. Only better.

'Had three or four seasons with Newport in the sixties. Bloody brilliant he was. Name in all the papers. Got himself a Welsh Trial. Could easily have played for Wales if he 'd really wanted to. But he was so bloody slap-happy. And sex mad. Such a lazy sod. They all gave him up in the end. Like Cousin Rupert you remember. "They thought so much about him, They did always play without him." So he moved away and ended up with us. But that's Anty all over. Indolent so-and-so.'

He shook his head. Gave Anty a withering look. Poured him another whisky. Pulled me a pint. And refilled his own glass.

'Poncey bastard he was when he played here, Rich. Never on time. Couldn't keep his hands off the women. Married or single. Didn't seem to matter to him. Always in trouble with some female. Or her jealous partner. Regular Don Jewan, he was. And absolutely stuffed with macho crap on the field. Designer stubble, skin-tight shorts, carryin' the ball in one hand, swallow divin' over the line. God, he used to make me puke.'

He pursed his lips in mock disgust.

Anty smiled. His special attractive smile. The one that made him look a bit like Jack Nicholson. The one, I guessed, that he still used to knock the ladies over.

'You're just jealous, Ronnie. You know the girls used to love it. That's what they came to see. There were more on the touchline out there when I was on the field, than I bet you've had in a month of Sundays since then. They just liked the way I played. I know they did. Because they said so. Dozens of 'em. "Beautiful hands you've got Anty" they were always telling me. "And hmmmm, those long, long touches you find. Right on the spot every time. Wonderful. And talk about being big on the burst. Ooh lovely"'.

He hooted.

'And you remember who my biggest fan was, don't you?'

He looked expectantly at my uncle.

'Can't say I do.' Uncle R was examining his second pint of bitter.

'Come on, Ronnie. Don't give me that. Course

you remember. Grace of the Green Lion. The one with the well developed personality. And the big Bristols. You know.

"Oh darling Grace
I love your face
I love you in your nightie
When the moonlight flits
Across your tits
Oh Jesus Christ Almighty.'"

Even Uncle R couldn't suppress a giggle.

'You old sod,' he said, 'you don't improve with age do you? But here's to you anyway.'

We drank to our mutual good health.

My uncle put his empty glass on the counter.

'Trouble with you, Anty, was you had so many of 'em. Like bleedin' flies round a cow pat they were. You weren't called the Mellstock Stud for nothing you know. Always damn well at it. We used to wonder sometimes how you had the energy to play rugby at all.

'What about that student nurse, for example? The one who looked after you in the Infirmary the time you got that knock on the head in the Grantley game. How long ago would it be now? Probably thirty-five years this comin' Saturday. But I remember it as if it were yesterday.'

Anty looked puzzled.

'Don't come it.' Uncle R turned to me again.

'He knows very well whom I'm talkin' about, Rich. He may have been Mellstock's answer to Don Jewan. But I bet he hasn't forgotten her.'

He prodded Anty on his silk handkerchief.

'It was that big wing forward Grantley had at the time. He clocked you in a late tackle. Got himself sent off for it. While you went wanderin' about the pitch talkin' absolute gibberish. Even worse than the codswallop you usually spouted on the field.

'We tried to tell the ref it was nothing unusual. You were often like that durin' a game. Due to those tight shorts you insisted on wearin'. They tended to cut off the blood supply to the organ that dominated your thinkin'. But he insisted you had concussion and sent you straight off to hospital.'

Uncle R paused for further refreshment.

'I popped into the Infirmary that evenin' about nine, Rich. To see if the old bugger was OK. And whether he needed anythin'. But I needn't have bothered. He was and he didn't.

'The little stoat had not only wangled himself a side-room on his own, but a really sexy young night nurse to look after him into the bargain. I caught 'em virtually at it. She said she was givin' him an injection. But it seemed to me more like the other way round.'

He put his tongue in his cheek and twitched his eyebrows.

Anty laughed.

'Just your dirty mind, Ronnie. Remember what I always say. To the pure in thought all things are pure.'

'Oh yeah.' Uncle R grinned a superior grin. 'But what about the other time you were carted off to the old boneshop. That game in Bristol. Against Hotwells Harlequins. When you did one of your bloody stupid swallow dives scorin' a try. And we all thought you'd broken your bleedin' neck. What about that then? All that palaver with the neck splints. And you moanin' and whimperin' fit to bust when they shoved you into the ambulance.'

He shook his head as he collected up our glasses and refreshed them yet again.

'What a performance, Rich. When we left for home that evenin' there was still no news from the hospital. And the word on the bus was that our master shafter had shot his last hole in one, and was well on the way to paraplegia.

'We should have known better.

'I telephoned the hospital when we got back to Mellstock, ready to hear the worst. And some tight-assed casualty sister informed me curtly that a Mr Youngman of Mellstock had been discharged a couple of hours earlier with nothin' more than a slight touch of torticollis.

'And guess what, Rich? When we got the full story a few days later, It turned out that old lecherous layabout here had been taken back to her place by a nubile young casualty nurse goin' off duty. So that she could spend her weekend treatin' his neck. While he spent his treatin' her kindly.

'Talk about away games. More like havin' it away games if you ask me.'

Delighted with his little pun, Uncle R polished off the last of his beer and kindly indicated that I might have the privilege of refilling his glass.

I refilled all three.

Our visitor topped up his Johnnie Walker with a splash of soda.

'Sorry, Ronnie,' he said, raising his glass in apology. 'I know I must have been a sex mad pain in the ass in those days. But they were bloody marvellous days nonetheless. We'll never see their like again. More's the pity. Best days of our lives, Ronnie. Best days of our lives. Here's to them. OK?'

'Ok, Anty, you old bugger you. OK.'

My uncle raised his glass in return. And we drank a second toast to our mutual health.

Anty looked pensive.

'I'll tell you one thing about those good old days, Ronnie. Something I've thought about a lot all these years I've been away. And that is that the best of them by far for me were those I spent with Grace from the Green Lion. What a great girl she was. And what a looker. Girl in a thousand. Wouldn't you agree?'

Uncle R nodded assent.

'Absolutely, you old stoat. Wonderful girl. We all thought you were bloody lucky to have her. Couldn't understand what she saw in an old shagnasty like you. But she was obviously pretty keen. The pair of you must have been shacked up together for a couple of years or more, weren't you?'

'At least that. And we probably still would be today, Ronnie, If I hadn't found out about her lover-boy.'

Anty looked mournful.

'What lover-boy? Don't tell me you had a rival !'

Uncle R grinned.

Anty nodded.

'I'd had my suspicions for some time. Came back to the flat once or twice and thought I could smell pipe smoke. Phone would ring and when I picked it up no-one would answer. Found a pair of men's yellow socks in the dirty laundry basket. She said they were her brother's. And then one night I turned up unexpectedly and caught the pair of 'em in bed together.'

'Really? Actually havin' it off?' Uncle R was intrigued. 'Who was he? Anyone I know?'

Anty shook his head.

'No idea. I never found out. The bugger got away too fast. Shinned down the drainpipe and was gone. And Grace would never tell me. So like a clod, I took the huff. And buggered off. We parted and that was that. Never saw her again. Never spoke to her. Never set foot in the Green Lion. She left Mellstock not all that long afterwards. And a couple of years later I heard she'd got married. To a Grantley player somebody said. Probably that big flank forward who flattened me a year or two earlier. The bastard.'

He gazed soulfully into his whisky.

'Biggest mistake of my life, leaving Grace. Stupidest thing I've ever done. And that's certainly saying something. As you know better than most, Ronnie. Still. Water under the bridge now, eh Ronnie? Water under the bridge.'

Uncle R, too, sat pensive for a moment.

'Ye-es,' he said slowly, 'Water under the bridge indeed. But you're right, Anty. She was a lovely girl. Lovely.'

He shook his head. And clapped his old friend on the shoulder.

'But nothin' much you can do about it now, old

man. Not after all these years. So best forget it. Let's have another drink. My shout.'

'Not for me, Unk,' I said, 'I'm just going for a pee. And then I've got to be getting home.'

'I'll come with you,' my uncle said 'To the pee-house I mean. Not home. Hang on a minute, Anty.'

Our visitor and I shook hands.

'See you at the match on Saturday,' he smiled.

'Nice chap,' I said to Uncle R as we stood side by side in the loo. 'Although I must say I'm a bit surprised that he's still fussing about that barmaid from the Green Lion and her phantom lover after all this time. God, it must be thirty years ago now.'

'More,' said Uncle R. 'Partly wounded pride, I suppose. The great Mellstock stud havin' his whatsit put out of joint by some pleb.'

He paused for a second.

'Although I must admit, I hadn't realised the lecherous old sod actually loved the girl.'

Something in his tone made me turn and take a closer look at him.

There was a decided twinkle in those little cockerel eyes of his. But his smile, although smug, had something rueful about it.

We zipped up and went to wash our hands.

'Unk, you old so and so. You know who the chap was, don't you? You've known all along.'

'As it happens I do and I have, Rich.'

'It was you wasn't it?'

His smile broadened.

'Modesty forbids, Rich,' he said. 'Modesty forbids.'

Chapter 14

Anty Redivivus

On the day of the Grantley match, I got to the Mellstock ground early. Deliberately. I'd telephoned my uncle the previous evening to see if he'd like a hand with any last-minute clearing up the following morning. But he wasn't interested.

'Thanks, Rich, but no thanks. Kind of you to offer.'

He became all schmaltzy.

'Call me a soppy old tart if you like. But I see it as a privilege to be allowed to clean up the Mellstock pavilion on the day all my old comrades in arms are flockin' here for their annual visit. So I do it as a personal tribute to them and to the DOC. After all I am...'

'DOC, Unk?' I interjected. 'Pardon me for interrupting your flow. But what the hell's the DOC?'

He gave a heavy sigh.

'Ignorant little toad. What else could it be but Dear Old Club? I ask you. Stupid bloody question. But as I was sayin' – After all I am the...'

'Denominazione d'Origine Controllata,' I muttered. 'Doctor On Call. District Officer Commanding. Department of Commerce. Daft Old Coot. Dissolved Organic Car...'

'Stop it,' he screeched. 'OK. I stand corrected. I was wrong. DOC can stand for other things as well. I accept that. But all I'm tryin' to say, if you'd only bloody well let me, is that as the club's official bar custodian, I reckon it's my duty to see the pavilion's kept clean and tidy. And tomorrow, because it's old boys' day, I've got this daft idea I'd like to do that duty all on my tod. No offence Rich, but that's the way it is. Comprendez?'

'Comprendez perfectly bueno, Unk. And no offence taken, I assure you. See you in the morning.'

I arrived just after noon. Uncle R had obviously been hard at it since the crack of dawn. The pavilion was cleaner and tidier than I'd ever seen it before. It even smelled different.

I soon found out why. I came upon my uncle in the lavatories, done up in overalls and green wellies, wandering like a houseproud maiden aunt, delicately perfuming each stall from a spray canister labelled "Spring Woodlands."

'Morning, Unk,' I said, 'Nice job you've done here. Any way I can help with the finishing touches? Get you some nice knitted toilet-roll covers perhaps? Polish up your ballcocks? Whitewash the coal?'

To my surprise he didn't seem amused.

'Not now, Rich. Not now. Highly droll, I agree. But not just now. I've been here since seven. And I'm knackered. So pardon me if I don't laugh out loud. Instead, maybe you'd like to make yourself useful by stickin' one of these in every cubicle. While I go and get myself cleaned up. OK?'

He stuck a large brown envelope into my hand,

and marched off grumbling in his beard.

I gave two fingers to his vanishing back.

'OK, you surly old sod,' I said to myself. 'Pardon me for living, I'm sure.'

But as ever he was one step ahead of me. He'd known from the moment he hung up his telephone the previous evening that I'd come to the ground early no matter what he said. And he'd obviously hung on to his "Spring Woodlands" spray, and the big brown envelope until I got there.

I emptied the envelope's contents into my hands. And found myself holding six drawing pins and six large, typewritten cards.

I did as he asked. Pinned a card in every WC.

Each cubicle now had a notice which read:

'Please don't throw your fag-ends down the pan. It makes them so difficult to smoke afterwards.'

'You crafty old bugger,' I said. Grinning. And made my way to the bar to seek him out.

But I was too late. Divested of his 'Dan, Dan The Lavatory Man' outfit, he was revealed in his idea of what the well-dressed rugby man wears on special occasions – tartan shirt, different pattern tartan tie, one of his better Fair Isle pullovers (baggy but not tattered) and ancient khaki corduroys. He was already pulling pints for the first half dozen of the Golden Oldies.

I decided to catch him later. As it turned out – it was much later.

The afternoon was damp. The Mellstock pack destroyed the Grantley scrum. Mellstock won in a canter. And the old contemptibles were back in the bar by four. Jubilant, and ready for the real business of the day, they applied themselves to non-stop booze and nostalgia, interspersed with rounds of cheese and pickle sandwiches, until well after ten. Then the whole gang of them, drunk as lords and merry as crickets, departed en bloc in search of the nearest Chinese take-away.

I found Uncle R, alone in the empty pavilion, standing behind the bar, a fixed smile on his face, swaying gently as he fed dirty glasses into the washer. The moment for our chat had at last arrived. I gathered up the rest of the empties, stacked them on the counter and collapsed onto a bar stool.

'Well, Unk, if there's one thing your old buddies certainly can do – it's drink. They shifted more booze today, in one afternoon and evening, than the whole of the rest of the club does in a month. You ought to get 'em to come more often. They'd do the bar takings a power of good.

'And talk about talk. I've never heard anything like it. Non-stop from the moment they arrived to the time you saw 'em off the premises. What a performance.'

I broke off for a second or two.

'Assuming of course, that you happen to be interested in old wrinklies who played rugby half a century ago.'

I grinned at my uncle and hurried on before he could explode.

'Which as you know, Unk, I very definitely am. Indeed I was quite looking forward to shaking the hand of the great Dai 'Arms Park' Davies today. And having another chat with your old pal Anty. But did I blazes. Dai didn't turn up. And Anty left early.

'I only caught sight of him once. Just before the match started. He was deep in conversation with a rather prissy looking bloke and a big, blonde woman. Bit on the blousy side for my taste. But obviously had once been quite a looker. And from the way he was ogling her – very much up Anty's alley. After the game there was no sign of him. Or the blonde and her prissy partner. Any idea who they were?'

Uncle R's face dissolved into a sly grin.

'George Gates and his wife Pam. He's Treasurer of Grantley. She's his second wife. Used to be his secretary. Twenty years younger than him. Bit of a flighty bint. Not short of a bob or two either. Came into a packet when her mother died. And you're right. Just Anty's cup of tea. But not only that. I reckon she could do with somethin' a bit livelier than old, stick-in-the-mud Georgie Porgie as well.'

He nodded sagely.

'So it wouldn't surprise me one little bit if the pair of 'em decided to buzz off together. Do a runner. Fold their tents like the God-damn Ayrabs and silently slip away for a life of luxury and unending how's yer father. Just like Anty did four years ago. With that other blonde piece. History doin' a bit of the old ditto repeato, Rich.'

He tapped his nose and looked knowing.

I raised my eyebrows.

'Anty and Madam Pearly Gates Unk? Never.'

'Why not?'

'Well. For one thing she's at least twenty years

younger than him. Secondly he's only just this minute met her. And thirdly she's well and truly married to old stuffed-shirt George.'

'So what? The previous one was thirty years younger than he was. And married with two kids. But that didn't stop him. Within a couple of weeks of first clappin' eyes on each other they'd buggered off together. Without a word to anybody. And I know that for a fact. 'Cos I was with him the day they met. In that little village supermarket out on the Hinton Road. She was the check-out girl. Betty her name was. Lovely bit of crumpet I can tell you. Long blonde hair. Great big Bristols. Legs up to her ass. Come-to-bed eyes. And saucy with it.'

His left eye wobbled lasciviously at the thought. And his hand shook alarmingly as he turned to stack the clean glasses on the shelves.

'We were on our way back from a county game over at Clampton when Anty suddenly decided he needed to stop and get a few groceries. Funnily enough right outside Betty's shop. Neither of us had ever set foot in the place before. But obviously a friend had tipped Anty the wink as to what was on offer inside.

'He walked straight up to the check-out counter, stuck out his hand, and without blinkin' an eyelid announced – "Hullo. You're the beautiful Betty, I presume. I've heard a lot about you. My name's Dick. Rod Dick. And I'm lookin' for a bit of hot stuff. Have I come to the right place?"

'She had a real cupid's bow pair of lips, Rich. Big. Pouty. All succulent and shiny. And a smile sort of lazy, warm and invitin'. And a very suggestive way of lookin' at you with those come-to-bed eyes. Sort of sultry. With the lids half-closed.

'She gave Anty the full treatment. And I could see immediately that he was a goner. He gazed at her like a male rattlesnake viewing a buxom young female white mouse.

"'Rod Dick," she said. "What a lovely name. So expressive. So full of hidden promise. And what do you want this hot stuff for, Rod? To warm up your widder's reminders?"

'She spoke slowly, with a seductive West Country burr. Like Jolene in The Archers.

"'Widder's reminders?"

'Anty looked puzzled.

"'Sausages, me old dear. Bangers. Pork Polonies."

'He gave her his Jack Nicholson grin.

"'Exactly. I want somethin' to perk up my pork polony lunch box. Maybe you can suggest somethin'?"

"'Mustard,' she said without battin' an eyelid, 'a nice big, dollop of mustard. For a man who looks pretty well mustard himself if you don't mind me sayin' so, I reckons it's just the thing you need. 'Omeopathic you might say."

'He leaned closer to her.

"'OK then, nurse. Whatever you say. I'm placing myself entirely in your hands. Do with me what you will. Let the dog see the mustard."

'He gave her the big eye.

"'What sort of mustard?" she enquired blandly. "English or Deejohn? 'Powder or ready-made? Tin, tube, or pot? Whole grain or smooth? Small, medium, large, family or jumbo?"

'She twitched her eyebrows.

'"Whatever you think appropriate Betty. Whatever you think will turn me on."

'She grinned.

'"Coleman's," she said, "that'll perk up any man's sausage."

'She slipped from her stool and took his arm.

'"Come on, lover. Over here. I'll show you everything I've got that might interest you."

'They vanished between the shelves at the back of the shop. I settled myself on the check-out counter and indulged in a little light reading matter from the magazine rack.

'Ten minutes later, when I'd finally finished my studies of 'Girls On Top' and was half-way through a careful perusal of 'Ladies Night At The Turkish Baths' – they reappeared.

'Anty had completed his supermarket business. In his basket lay a small tube of Coleman's English Mustard.

'Betty gave his shoulder a playful squeeze.

'"Come into my office, lover, and I'll just check out your goods."

'"Certainly Nurse Betty," he said, "At your cervix."

'"Oooh, Mr Dick.' She put a coy hand to her lips and flashed him a cheeky smile. "Dilated I'm sure."

'They hooted with libidinous laughter.

'Two weeks later, Rich, they'd both vanished into the wild blue yonder. And they haven't been seen since until Anty suddenly reappeared at the club a couple of days ago. What they've been up to all this time nobody really knows. Although there's been plenty of suggestions believe you me.

'Half the club claims to know for a fact that they were runnin' everythin' from a sweet shop in Horley to a whore shop in Sweetley. And dozens of members reckon that one or other of 'em had been seen drivin' a bus, a lorry, a van, a minicab, and even a tractor. Sellin' insurance, brushes, women's underwear, dirty postcards, mechanical mice, Gameboys, the Big Issue, their bodies. Livin' in every known place from Aberystwyth to York, And in every known sort of accommodation – lodging house, country house, public house, doss house, bawdy house and squat.

'In other words, Rich, they were here, there, everywhere and nowhere. And nobody had a bleedin' clue as to where they actually were, or what they were actually doin'.

'So if the Mellstock stud and randy Pam really have pushed off together, if it's history ditto repeato, as I'm seriously suggestin' it is, then I reckon we won't see hide nor hair of either of 'em again for a long, long time. Could be years. You wait and see, young Rich. I'll bet you a hundred quid to a penny, I'm right.'

I should have accepted the wager.

Within four months the voluptuous Pam was back in Mellstock. Insisting that the long break she'd just spent in the West Indies with a distant cousin, had been fabulously, romantically, idyllicly, wonderful. But though her tan supported her story, the sour, disappointed, shrewish cast of her face did not.

If fifteen weeks in the Caribbean realising love's young dream left you with a look like that, the general view suggested, you'd be better off staying at home. And up and down Mellstock the speculation on the street centred not on where she had been and with whom. But on which of the Caribbean's many islands Anty had dumped her for something younger and more interesting.

And as for her callous and unfeeling s-h-one-t of a lover, his reappearance was delayed for a little longer. Sixteen months longer to be exact.

The Millenium came and was three-quarters gone when Uncle R and I were taking our ease, one warm autumn evening, under the wide open windows of the Mellstock pavilion bar. He in his favourite decrepit old armchair. I, flaked out on the equally decrepit, adjacent sofa. Between us, on the floor, stood my uncle's trusty, one gallon, enamel beer jug. Before us, on a low table, stood the club's best television set. We were idly watching a rerun of the opening ceremony of the Sydney Olympics.

To be quite honest, the string of parading teams and the gentle burbling of the commentators had already lulled me into a light doze. And I thought it had done the same for Uncle R. But obviously not. For suddenly he burst out with an explosive curse.

'Well bugger me sideways. It's him. Rich ! Rich ! Wake yourself up lad. It's him. It's the stud himself. Large as life and lookin' a thousand dollars. The old bastard. It's Anty. For God's sake. It's Anty.'

I gazed at the screen where his finger was pointing. Somewhere between Romania and South

Africa. Just coming up to the VIP dais. It was him all right. Immaculate in white. Shoes, suit and tropical trilby. Grinning all over his face. Carrying a vast yellow, green and pale blue flag that matched his tie. And leading a team of fifteen contestants, all dressed exactly the same as him, except that they all wore skirts.

The commentator seemed enlivened by their appearance. They were clearly media pets.

'And here come the team that the spectators have already taken to their hearts,' he announced. 'Probably the smallest national squad in the whole games. From the tiny Caribbean island of St Agnes. Fifteen swimmers and divers. All girls. All beautiful. All raring to go. And all led by the man – lucky chap – whom I gather is their manager, trainer, guide, philosopher, friend, inspiration and father figure. An Englishman from Mellstock – Arthur Youngman. Who tells me that although a highly experienced swimming coach, his real love is rugby in which, some years ago, he got a trial for Wales.'

Anty and his girls, still one huge dusky smile, marched out of our screen.

Uncle R sat there with his mouth open. One of the few times I ever saw him at a loss for words.

Finally he found his voice.

'Highly experienced swimmin' coach, my ass. Lyin' little sod. He was bloody useless in the water. Swam like a bleedin' stone. If someone's been turnin' those girls into world-beaters in the pool, it certainly isn't him. Although I bet he's done his best to satisfy all their other burnin' desires. Dirty little devil.'

He shook his head in disbelief.

'But isn't it typical of Anty. Pisses off with Randy Pam. Gets her to finance him back to the West Indies. Dumps her. And instead of turnin' into a beach bum, somehow wangles his way into becomin' manager, coach and grand panjandarum to an all-girl national swimmin' team. It's bloody unbelievable. The man could fall down a sewer and still come up smellin' of roses.'

I grinned at him.

'Would I be right in assuming you're suffering a bit from the presence of the old green-eyed monster, Unk?'

He grinned back.

'You would, Rich. You would. But not a bit. A bloody great dose, I assure you. Who wouldn't be? King of a coral island stuffed to the gunwales with wonderful Caribbean crumpet. All of which thinks you're some kind of English superman. And want to spend their lives givin' you pleasure. Sounds like the nearest thing to heaven I'm ever likely to come across on this earth. So, yes. Of course. I certainly am envious of Anty. Bloody envious. Lucky old sod that he is. God damn him.'

He paused, emptied his tankard and refilled us both.

'And you know what he's gonna do now, Rich, don't you?'

He started to laugh out loud.

'Win a couple of Olympic gold medals. That's what.'

I laughed with him.

'Never in a hundred years, Unk. Not with the Aussies and the Yanks around. Take it from me. He and those girls of his haven't got a prayer.'

Which, only goes to show how wrong you can be. Come the end of Games, St Agnes returned home with two golds, a silver and two bronzes. Anty, we learned later, was granted the freedom of the island, national citizenship, and a pension for life. We've never seen him since.

Chapter 15

The Peahen And The KO

Uncle R was standing in the bay window of the bar, gazing out at the first fifteen pitch. He was smiling. He'd had good news.

About the KO. It was back in business. Saved by an anonymous benefactor. Some madass rugby fancier with a heart of gold and a wallet to match.

For every quid raised by the clubs entering the annual Hospital Cup knock-out competition, he was ready to donate a tenner.

My father was delighted. The Mellstock Royal Infirmary got all the proceeds. And he was its secretary.

My Uncle was equally chuffed. He'd moaned and groaned for the past twelve months about the KO's demise.

'After a hundred bloody years, Rich, the stupid buggers let it die. Can you Adam and Eve it. I ask you. It survives two world wars and God knows how many national disasters. From the Great Depression to professional rugby. And then dies from lack of interest.

'It would serve the local clubs' right if we all sat back and let it stay dead. But that ain't gonna happen. Not to the KO. Your father and I are gonna make sure of that.'

'How?' I'd asked him.

He'd looked at me pityingly.

'Elementary, my dear Richard. First we'll find an angel. Second we'll give the chairmen of the local clubs the little bit of special encouragement they badly need.'

'And what sort of encouragement would that be, Unk?' I'd grinned.

'Guess.' He'd grinned back.

'Something to do with winkle-picker shoes and jaxies perhaps?'

His grin had turned devilish.

'Spot on, Rich. Spot on.'

And so they did.

They shamed, blamed and generally gingered up the local clubs. And then, from the massed ranks of their old cronies they dug up a genuine, 18 carat, gold-plated angel.

I approached the Mellstock pavilion the morning after the resurrection of the KO was announced. I could see Uncle R standing in the window of the bar. He saw me through the glass.

'Come on in, Rich,' he shouted. 'There's a pint here with your name on it. And a toast waiting to be drunk.'

Pint glass against two-pint tankard, we clinked and drank to the KO – its rejuvenation and future well-being.

That done, Uncle R resumed his study of the first fifteen pitch outside the window.

'Of course,' he said, still standing with his back to

me. 'This isn't the first time the KO's been in deep crapola. It nearly went down the tubes thirty-odd years ago.'

'How so?' I enquired.

'Same reason. Lack of bloody interest by the clubs and the local populace. In a way, your father helped save the day that time as well.'

He paused and emptied his tankard.

'Haven't I ever told you about it?' he said over his shoulder. 'One of the strangest games of rugby I've ever played in.'

'In which you ever played, Unk.' I suggested pedantically. Grinning at his back. 'No, you never have.'

'Smartass,' he said without turning his head. 'And take that silly grin off your face if you want another pint.'

I carried on grinning.

'Sorry, Unk. No offence meant.'

'None taken.' He went behind the bar and drew off two pints of best.

'It was the KO final of 1965. I was gettin' a bit long in the tooth. But I was still playin'. Not for Mellstock that day. They hadn't entered. So I'd been guestin' for MUMs. You know. Mellstock United Methodists. Their ground was right next door to where I lived then.'

He took a swallow and smacked his lips.

'We were playin' the holders in the final. Bell Green Old Boys. Clangers, as everyone insists on calling 'em. A rough old lot in those days. Kick everythin' above grass. And don't be afraid to hand out a few knuckle sandwiches. That was their basic game plan. Get your retaliation in first. And don't get the ball out to your wingers if you're more than fifteen yards from your opponent's line.

'To call it dull is bein' charitable, Rich. It was diabolically, brain-numbingly dreary. But it had won them the cup seven years on the trot.

'Which is why your father was gettin' really worried.

'It had all become too predictable, you see. Clangers had been top dogs for so long everyone was losing interest. Some clubs didn't even bother to enter any more. Supporters – except for Clangers' supporters – had become apathetic. Collections collapsed. Donations dwindled. And your dad reckoned that the Bell Green boys only had to win one more time and the whole shebang would self-destruct out of utter boredom.

'So he decided the time had come to warn everyone concerned at the MRI of the likely loss of one of their oldest, regular, annual sources of income. Small though the total KO takings were compared with a year's running costs at the Infirmary. Twenty or thirty thousand towards a bill of millions. It was a big morale booster for the staff. Especially for those who usually benefitted from the donation. Like the Peahen.

He raised his eyebrows and regarded me expectantly.

I decided to indulge him.

'OK, Unk. I'll buy it. Who the hell was the Peahen?'

'The Casualty Sister at the MRI Rich. Sister Penelope Pocock to give her her proper name. But to two generations of Mellstock rugby players, the Peahen.

'Big as any second row forward. Bossy as an RSM. Tender as a kitten. She had taken us, and our fathers before us, into her department by the ambulance-load. Mended our bodies, bones or brains. Whatever was broken. And sent us home better.

'To a man we regarded her with a mixture of fear, respect and affection. And then laughed like drains behind her back at her little-girl voice, the fact that she couldn't pronounce her rs, and her unendin', unintentional double-entendres.

'As for her, individually, I'm sure she loved and cosseted every last one of us rugby lads. But collectively we got on her wick. Somethin' she never tired of makin' clear to your father whenever he came her way. More than once when I was receivin' attention myself and he came over to see how thin's were goin', I heard her moanin' away at him.

"Januawy, Febwuawy and March, when theyah playing that fwightful Hospital Cup, Mr Cwoss. Theyah fwaught, absolutely fwaught for my gels and me. All those dweadful wugby injuwies. Why, the demands all those young KO boys make on our wesauces are enawmous. Weah ovahwhelmed Mr Cwoss. Completely ovahwhelmed. We just can't satisfy them. It's widiculous.'

'And your dad always took her seriously, Rich. Never the ghost of a grin. Not from the master of the hidden smile. Mr Diplomacy himself. No. He would listen, sympathise, and remind her yet again how much Casualty had benefitted down the years from cash provided by the KO.

'So of course, as the final of the competition drew nearer for what he really believed would be the very last time, he felt duty-bound to tell her of its approachin' doom.

"'I'm not quite sure how you're going to react to what I have to tell you, Sister.'"

She looked suspicious.

"'Weally, Mr Cwoss. But neither of us will know until you explain what it is will we. So pahaps you'd bettah spit it out."

"'Well I thought I ought to let you know that this coming Final of the Hospital Cup competition may well be the very last we'll ever see."

'She frowned.

"'For what weason, Mr Cwoss?"

"'There is a team in the KO Cup, Sister, called Bell Green Old Boys."

"'I'm puhfectly awaeh of that, Mr Cwoss. Clangahs, you mean. An extremely wough team so I'm told. Half the wugby injuwies that come into my Casualty seem to be caused by them."

"'Yes, Sister, Clangers. Well, they've won the competition now for the last seven years. And everyone is getting bored and fed up with it. No suspense. No surprise. Everybody knows before the tournament even starts, exactly how it's going to end.

"'So there's less and less interest. And less and less interest means less and less money for us. So unless there's a miracle this year and Clangers lose, I think the KO will just fade out. Takin' at least half of our annual budget for smaller items of new equipment with it."

'The Peahen looked pensive. Every year a chunk of the expected KO takings were earmarked for new equipment in the Casualty Department.

"'I see," she fluted, 'and who are the Clangahs playing in the final, Mr Cwoss?"

"'Mellstock United Methodists, Sister. MUMs, as they're called. And although my brother Ronnie who's turning out for them this year wouldn't necessarily agree with me, to my mind they haven't got a cat's chance in hell of winning. Sadly."

"'Youah shuah, Mr Cwoss? The MUMs have no hope of beating those howwid Clangahs people. None at all?"

"'Not a sausage Sister. Unless, as I said, some kind of miracle takes place. And that would be asking too much, wouldn't it."

'He placed a comforting hand on her ham-like arm.

"'Well, Mr Cwoss." The Peahen had been silent for a few moments, digesting the bad news.

"'We have obviouly weached cwisis point. Something special must be done. We must all wally wound. Put on ouah thinking caps. And do ouah vewy best to help the MUMs give those Clangahs wotters a weally sound thwashing. I shall have to have a pow-wow with my gels and see what we can do.

"'Wemembah Mr Cwoss. Nil Despewandum. Miwacles do sometimes happen. So keep youah peckah up."

'She patted your dad's arm in return and vanished back into the depths of Casualty.

'Your father stood silent for a while. Then returned gloomily to the papers on his desk.

Chapter 16

The Final

We were on our third pint. Uncle R had finally given up gazing at the first fifteen pitch and joined me at the bar.

'And by the way, Rich, if you're wonderin' how I know so much about your dad's dealin's with his Casualty Sister thirty years ago, the answer's simple. He reported 'em all to me at the time.

'The two of us have always been pretty close as you know. None of that sibling rivalry crap between us. And in those days we used to meet two or three times a week after work for a couple of pints and an exchange of gossip. Usually in what used to be the Infirmary's favourite pub. The Fox and Hen in Bridge Street.

'That's where I remember us both laughing out loud when he told me about the Peahen's promise to "wally wound," "pow-wow with her gels," and produce a plan to "give those Clangahs wotters a weal thwashing in the KO Final." And that's where, on the evenin' before the Final itself, we sat and drank a solemn toast to a MUMs victory the followin' day. More in hope than expectation I must admit, Rich. With your dad lookin' about as optimistic as a depressive on death row.

'The next afternoon he looked much the same. More like a man attendin' a funeral than a rugby match. I caught sight of him in the crowd as I trotted out onto the pitch with the rest of the MUMs side. The opposition were already there. And so was the Peahen and her gels. Unmistakeable on the touchline with their long, blue, nurses' capes turned inside out to show their red linin's.

'Clangers were a real sight for sore eyes. They had obviously fallen for all the crap that had appeared in the Mellstock Echo about them bein' the bad boys of local rugby. And had started to act the part.

'They slouched about, scowlin', sneerin' and generally givin' the impression of blokes racked with chronic constipation. And they'd all had their hair done. Some were shaved bald. Some, punk pink and green. Some looked like the last of the Mohicans. Every one of the buggers had six-day beards. A couple had taken their teeth out. And all the forwards were vaselined up to the ears.

'And that wasn't the end of it, Rich. No sooner had we appeared on the pitch than they decided to put the real frighteners on us.

'They formed up facin' us, in a wide half-circle round the centre-spot, and started stampin' their feet, shakin' their fists, slappin' themselves about the head and body, glarin' like loonies and gruntin' like bleedin' warthogs.

'When we got over our surprise, we realised they were snortin' their way through some nonsensical Mellstockian version of the All Blacks' Haka.

'Led by their captain, a big second-row forward

called Digger O'Dowd. Eyes poppin' like mad bulls. Tongues wagglin' like rattlesnakes. They urrghed and aarghed themselves up to a huge war cry, bellowed out as they made a final, arm-wavin' leap into the air.

'Obviously delighted with their performance, they muscled their way back to their kick-off positions. While we burst out laughin', Rich. We couldn't help it. They looked and sounded so bloody ridiculous. So we gave 'em a spontaneous round of applause. Which made the crowd cheer, the Clangers look surprised and suspicious, and the whole of the MUMs team grin like hyenas.

'As a result we kicked-off in a sort of euphoric haze. Cheerful as crickets. Mad as coots. We'd suddenly decided that the last thing we were goin' to do that afternoon was lie down and let these poncey plods trample all over us.

'So we didn't. Anyway not in the first half.

'For forty minutes we stood toe to toe, eyeball to eyeball, and slugged it out with 'em. Anythin' they gave us, we returned with interest. Jabs, elbows, gouges, flyin' arkwrights, knuckle sandwiches, trips, groin grabbin', stampin', we traded the lot. If they showed us the five studs. We showed 'em all eight. And when they produced their secret weapon in the scrums – collective huffin' out of disgustin' garlic breath – we just gritted our teeth, held our noses and took it like men.

'So fired up were we by half-time, so enveloped in the old red mist, that some of us didn't even realise that we were actually in the lead, beneficiaries of a hatful of penalties arising from Clangers' thud and blunder, two of which our full-back kicked. Six points to love.

'But that was the first half. The second was a different story.

'Big, rough-cut, Digger O'Dowd had gathered his boys around him in the interval and torn a dozen strips off 'em. And as a result they came up with a completely different game plan after the break.

'They didn't cut out the rough stuff altogether. That would have been askin' too much. Like requestin' lions to pack in eatin' meat. But they did cut it down by at least fifty per cent. Spendin' less time kickin' us, and more puntin' the ball deep into our territory, so as to get close enough to our line to give their threes a run.

'And the tactics worked. They were inside our twenty-five a dozen times before the game ended. But they only scored one try.

'I'd like to say that it was our magnificent blanket defence that kept 'em out Rich. But I can't. Not if I'm honest.

'I said earlier on, didn't I, that that Final was one of the oddest games of rugby I ever played in. Well, let me tell you why.

'Havin' got their try and converted it, six points to five, and with about twenty minutes still left for play, they really did get on a roll,

'Four times they should have scored. But four times they cocked it up. Or should I say, Rich – four times it was cocked up for them.

'"The fanciful fumblings of the fickle finger of fate," as the Echo's rugby man – a great alliterator –

put it. And you can understand why.

'Take for example the two tries that Keith Slim almost scored.

'Keith was what you might call eponymous, Rich. He was exactly like his name. Tall and thin. Legs like a robin. And with his head shaved for the Final, he looked for all the world like a scootin' skeleton. But one thin' is certain. He couldn't half shift when he put his mind to it. And he put his mind to it twice in ten minutes in the last quarter of the game.

'But he didn't actually get the ball over the line on either occasion.

'The first time, he was clear away when he suddenly stopped dead on the twenty-five, as though he'd run into a brick wall. And our winger caught him up and knocked him for six, ball and all, into the crowd.

'The second time, about five minutes later, just when he seemed to be about to dive over the goal-line, he dived Assam over Elba straight into touch instead.

'We couldn't make head or tail of it. Stoned, we wondered? Or perhaps hittin' the sauce hard before the game was part of the new Clangers' image. But Keith insisted otherwise.

'"Someone in the crowd clobbered me with a bloody great hand-off," he moaned to the ref after the first run. "I know so, because I saw this bloody great ham-like arm shoot out and catch me right in the chops. The bastard. He was wearin' a blue shirt with white cuffs."

'And as for the second time, he was even more

forthright.

'"I was tripped,' he screamed, "some bugger here tripped me up with an umbrella. Or a stick. Or something. Dirty bugger."

'On each occasion, the referee did his best. First he cautioned Keith for usin' bad language on the field. Then he had a word with the crowd on the touchline. Especially with the Peahen and her gels. Who happened to be right on the spot both times. But nobody could confirm the hand-off story. And as for a stick or similar, none could be found – walkin', shootin', hockey, pogo, or sword.

'Then, Rich, there was the business of the lost balls. With time tickin' away, the Clangers' pack had a real kamikaze period, and drove us and the ball into touch right on our own corner flag. A quick throw-in and they were bound to score. But they couldn't throw in because there was no ball to throw.

'Some of the Peahen's gels standin' nearby helped the Clangers' wing look for it. But it was no good. It had completely vanished. Along with the two spares. And by the time someone had got a new one from the pavilion, their mad frenzy had evaporated, we'd got our breath back, and we managed to clear our line.

'Five minutes to go. The crowd goin' wild. And both teams pretty well exhausted.

'"Keep 'em out, MUMs. Keep 'em out" our supporters begged.

'"Drop one, Clangers. Drop one," their followers urged, desperate for a drop-goal.

'On the pitch it was stalemate. We'd literally fought our way to a standstill, Rich. And with only a couple of minutes left, were locked in a loose maul on our twenty-five. We were doin' our best to make sure we stayed there until the whistle went. Clangers' pack were too tired to do much about it. All except one.

'Big, rough-cut Digger O'Dowd, inspired by the sort of desperation known only to captains faced with the loss of a seven-year unbeaten record, made one, last, weary, superhuman effort to wipe out our one point lead.

'Rippin' out of the loose maul with the ball at his feet, he set off for the line. He had twenty-five yards to go and the match to win. And nobody was gonna stop him. Or so he thought.

'He wasn't dribblin' one ball anymore, but four'.

'But with only twenty-three yards behind him and

two still to cover, he suddenly discovered he wasn't dribblin' one ball anymore, but four.

'The three so strangely lost twenty minutes earlier, equally strangely suddenly reappeared from among the crowd, and our bacon was saved.

'All four balls shot over the goal-line. Our fullback dropped on two. Digger O'Dowd collapsed on another. Clangers' touch judge fell on the fourth. The crowd fell about laughin'. The ref fell back on a five-yard scrum. Defender's ball. We cleared to touch. And the game was over.

'Controversy raged for weeks. But our one-point victory stood. And interest in the KO rocketed as a result.'

Grinning like a Chinese idol, my uncle paused in his tale to draw us a fourth pint each.

'Clangers' president, of course, called for a replay, Rich. But after a special, extraordinary meetin' of the KO committee it was decided that the peculiar happenin's at the Final fell into the category of Acts of God, and so were beyond the committee's, or anyone else's jurisdiction.

'It was not God, however, whom I found your father toastin' in his office at the infirmary, when I called there on the evenin' of the match, to take him off to the Fox and Hen for a celebratory few beers.

'"To you, Sister Penelope," he was sayin', raisin' a glass of the hospital's best sherry to the Peahen. "And to your band of splendid Casualty nurses. Our humble and grateful thanks."

'It was possible, Rich, that he was referrin' to the takin's at that afternoon's match. Boosted by a special collection from a happy crowd after the game. Or he could have been toastin' the increased interest in the KO that our unexpected victory was bound to create. He might even have been thankin' the Casualty Sister and her gels for all the excellent repair work done on damaged rugby players throughout the season.

'But I don't think so. And neither obviously did the Peahen.

'She smiled coyly and raised her ham-like arm to clink her glass with his. She was wearin', I noticed, a blue dress with white cuffs.

'"How tewwibly, tewibbly kind of you, Mr Cwoss,' she trilled. 'We nurses do like to think that sometimes we have somethin' under ouah cloaks to please you wough, wugby men."

'For once Rich, your father forgot not to laugh.'

Chapter 17

The Victor Sylvester Of Mellstock

Uncle R was not in the best of humours. He never was when he was tending his roses. Not that they were really his roses. They'd stood along the front side of the Mellstock rugby pavilion for years. As sickly, diseased and stunted a row of bushes as persistent neglect could produce.

But recently he'd decided to do something about them. And wasn't finding the task easy.

This time the problem was clouds. They'd rolled up suddenly when he was right in the middle of spraying. And the thought of rain washing off the protective pesticide he was so busy putting on, had begun to shorten his temper even before I arrived with my query.

'Dances?' he snapped, 'What dances?'

He took his finger off the trigger of his spray gun, removed his disgusting old Panama hat, flicked the sweat from his eyebrows and fixed me with an accusing stare.

I shook my head sadly.

'Poor old devil,' I said, addressing the wizened remains of what had once been a handsome Fragrant Cloud. 'It must be a bit difficult for him, at his age, to remember something that's only been discussed by the rugby club committee at its last four meetings. Especially for a bloke, as Auntie Madge always says, who was born with two left feet.'

I gave him a sideways glance.

He took the opportunity to direct a squirt of his foul-smelling green liquid as close to my expensive new trainers as he could get.

'Don't come it,' he said, 'unless you'd like a few nice green spots on those poncey white sailor trousers as well. And don't believe everythin' your Aunt Madge tells you either. Wonderful woman. But poor old girl's memory's not what it was.'

'OK, Unk, point taken,' I said, 'and I'll let Auntie Madge know you've told me about her infirmity.'

He replaced the Panama and drew a bead on me with the spray gun.

'Not a word, lad. Not a dickie bird. Not if you're really fond of that shirt and tie you're wearin'. Pure cotton and woven silk if I ain't mistaken. Very nice. But not the sort of items you want green stains on eh? So what's it to be? Stumm and crum, or Jermyn Street's best up the Swanee? Your choice.'

I held up my hand. Grinning.

'OK, Unk. You win. Stumm it shall be. An oyster couldn't be stummer. No word of Auntie Madge's little trouble shall ever pass my lips. Promise.'

'I should hope so Rich. Because let me tell you that though you may not think so now, I was quite a hoofer in my day. Strictly ballroom of course. Man and woman stuff. None of this wankers away, solo crap. Couples movin' as one. Thigh to thigh. Hips really tight up together. Man leadin'. Woman followin'. Oooh aaagh.'

His eyelids flickered and his body quivered as he performed a couple of nondescript steps around a half-dead Elizabeth of Glamis.

'Yes. Nifty on the old trotters I was. Good at everythin' from the turkey trot to the paso doble. Ass wigglin' a speciality. They didn't call me the Victor Sylvester of Mellstock for nothin' you know.'

'Victor who, Unk?'

'Sylvester, Rich, you ignorant little bleeder. King of strict tempo. Lord of a thousand local Pallays de Dance. Master of the slow, slow, quick, quick, slow.'

'Really. Never heard of him. Dead now, I suppose.'

'As it happens he is Rich. But take it from me, the champion ballroom dancer of his day. The original Old Smoothie. Mr White Tie and Tails himself.'

'And you were his star pupil. Is that it?'

'Not exactly.'

The green spray wavered in my direction.

'But it was generally agreed around Mellstock in the forties and fifties that I gave the local dance floors some pretty good leather. Famous for my square tango, I was. All macho and sneerin'. Throwin' my partner about, and bendin' her over backwards 'til her head banged on the floor. Girls used to queue up for it. Talk about Snake Hips Johnson.'

He executed a clumsy double shuffle across the grass towards the pavilion steps. I skipped aside. The green liquid was going everywhere.

'OK, Snake Hips. So what about the disco evenings then?'

He stopped in his tracks.

'Disco evenin's. What disco evenin's?'

I snorted in frustration.

'The dances, Unk, for god's sake. The dances. The ones I asked you about ten minutes ago. The ones we've been discussing at the club committee for the past four months. Monthly discos in the pavilion for the next three months. With me as the DJ.'

I paused to breathe on the nails of my right hand and polish them ostentatiously on my shirt-front.

'Under my very own personal supervision, Unk. And you don't even remember they're taking place, do you? I must say that's hurtful. Very hurtful.'

I sighed deeply, and bowed my head, keeping a weather eye on his trigger finger as I did so.

I needn't have worried. Memories of his dancing days had smoothed away much of my uncle's irritation.

He adopted a pained expression and lifted his eyes skyward in silent reproach to God for saddling him with such a clown of a nephew.

'Lord almighty,' he said. 'Disco evenin's under your personal supervision, is it? And I've had the bleedin' temerity to let that vital bit of information slip my mind. Well pardon me for livin', I'm sure.'

His little cockerel eyes narrowed.

'But who can blame me, Rich? After all, what man in his right senses wouldn't do his utmost to block out of his mind the guts-turnin' thought of three teenage discos in three months. Nights of tuneless bleedin' crap. Ghastly, ear-splittin' mind-blowin' bloody noise. Flashin' lights blindin' everybody in sight. Adenoidal young turds shoutin' and bawlin' gibberish, and callin' it singin'. Kids wagglin' their asses all over the place. Havin' a half of lager shandy and screamin' about how terribly, terribly drunk they are. Or takin' some stupid bloody drug, havin' the vapours and passin' out in the bog. I should cocoa. God preserve me from bloody teenagers en masse.'

He gave a moribund Iceberg a vicious soaking.

'Come on, Unk,' I said, smiling at him. 'Be your age. Or rather don't be your age quite so much. Don't knock it 'til you've tried it. And anyway when have you ever let anyone else but you, run the bar at a club event? Remember, if you don't do it, we shall have to try and do it ourselves. Because there's no way these discos are gonna be cancelled now. They're in much too good a cause for that.'

He looked at me suspiciously.

'What good cause?'

'Helping to get the ladies' rugby section started, Unk. What better cause could there be?'

A look of horror spread over his face. His little eyes popped. His mouth fell open. Veins started throbbing in his neck and temples. His spray gun hand shook.

'Ladies' rugby section?' he said. Almost choking. 'You're tellin' me that all this hoo-ha is about settin' up a ladies' section here? At the Mellstock Club?'

For a brief moment I thought he was about to have an apoplectic fit.

'Females playin' rugby?' he said, shaking his head in disbelief. 'Girls playin' a man's game? Young – women – actually – strippin' off – and – playin'...' His voice trailed off. His hand steadied. The throbbing at his neck and temples subsided. His little, cockerel eyes were suddenly lit by a libidinous gleam.

'What a very good idea, Rich,' he said. 'Never thought of it before. But now you mention it – why not? If that's what they want – why not indeed. Can't be stick-in-the-muds, can we? Gotta move with the times. So if the little dears want to get out on the field in their flimsy little shorts and tight jerseys, I for one am not gonna stand in their way.

'Might even offer to give 'em a hand myself, Rich. Let 'em have the benefit of my experience. Become their trainer and coach perhaps. Look after 'em. Build 'em into a team. Give 'em tactical talks. One to one advisory sessions. Personal massage. Alcohol rubs. All that sort of thin'.'

His hand had started trembling again. There was movement once more in the veins about his head. The gleam in his cockerel eyes had become a lecherous leer.

I smiled as I thought of some of the prime movers in the push for a Mellstock Ladies rugby team. Lorna, the sixteen-stone, long-distance lorry driver. Big Phyllis, Jill of all trades on her father's farm in Grantley. Hurling the Wellie Champion of Mellstock and District these past three years. And her bosom pal, Roberta the Squirter, artificial inseminator supreme, and surrogate bull to a hundred cows a week in the Mellstock area. Anchors of the would-be Ladies XV scrum. Each one was quite capable of picking up my uncle with one hand while drinking off a yard of ale with the other.

'Good thinking, Batman,' I said, 'I'll let the girls know what you have in mind, and see how they react. They could easily fall on your neck, Unk.'

'My thoughts exactly, Rich. I think they'll appreciate havin' an older man to look after 'em. Someone who's been around. Who knows a thing or two. Someone who understands women as well as rugby. A father figure, who can talk to them man to man, like a Dutch uncle.'

'Absolutely, Unk. Takes a very unusual bloke to be able to do that. And you could be the very chap.'

He beamed. Laid down his spraying equipment on a nearby seat. Chucked his old Panama beside it. Took out a half-smoked pipe from his pocket. Put a match to it and perfumed the air with a stream of silver Erinmore smoke.

'Let's go and wet the old whistles Rich. I could do with a break. And I need to give a bit of thought to these disco dances. Specially if I'm gonna be guide, philosopher and bosom friend to this new girls' rugby side. They'll expect their coach to be with it on the old dance floor. Particularly a bloke with my reputation as a good little mover.'

He sashayed up the steps to the pavilion entrance: shoulders hunched, hands in the air, thick hips rotating, stomach wobbling, struttin' his stuff like some Calypso King at the Notting Hill Carnival.

'Goodbye Victor Sylvester,' he announced. 'Lookout Dirty Dancin'. Here I come.'

Eyes heavenward to beg him indulgence from a kindly Lord, I followed him in.

Chapter 18

The Rugby Ball

The bar still had that sour-sweet smell of the previous night's drinking. I perched myself on one of the stools at the counter and waited while my uncle vanished behind it, raised the shutter and sat down opposite me. The disco details, such as they were, were settled in seconds as he performed a cockpit check of his pipes, pumps and engines and drew off a couple of frothing trial quarter-glasses

Over our first pint he waxed reminiscent.

'No wonder my bloody dancin's a bit bloody rusty Rich. The club's only ever had one decent dance the whole time I've known it. We used to occasionally put on an impromtu hop in the pavilion. But they were crap. Bit like these disco nonsenses you've got in mind.'

He gave me a sideways glance to see if I'd rise to the bait. I ignored him.

'No. The only real dance we've had in years, with a proper band and all that, was the Rugby Ball. Fancy dress affair. Way back in the mid fifties. You'd have loved it. Right up your alley. Exhibitionist little sod like you.'

This time I took my cue.

'And right up yours too, Unk, if I may say so.

Otherwise why would you have remembered it after all these years? Must have made quite an impression.'

He smiled.

'You're right. It did, Rich. A lastin' impression. No doubt about that.'

His smile became enigmatic.

'So, tell me about it, Unk. To start with, what did you go as?'

'Me? Guess.'

'Wore your best suit and your Panama and went as a scarecrow?'

'Cheeky sod.'

'Jock strap and three-cornered hat as Big Dick Turpin?'

'Don't be filthy.'

'OK then. Cushion up the back of your jersey and a one-eyed mask as the Hunchback of Notre Dame?'

'Fool.'

'Took off the mask and went as the Beast from 10,000 Fathoms?'

'Saucy bugger.'

'What then?'

'Someone who was a real star in those days Rich. A real star. Not to your generation of course. I doubt if any of your lot've even heard of him. Ignorant little buggers that you are. But I thought he was bloody marvellous. Swallow-tail coat. Steel rimmed glasses. Bit of burnt cork. Big ceegar. King of the one-liners. Master Wisecracker. Groucho Marx. Mean anythin' to you?'

I looked at him as one might at an idiot child.

'Do me a favour, Unk. I absolutely adore that

man. And so, I can assure you, do dozens more of what you like to call "my lot" in Mellstock. Surely you know the Marx Brothers've got a thriving fan club here. Hundreds of members of all ages. Meets regularly in that big room above the Turk's Head. And has special screenings of all their films. They're cult movies now, for God's sake. I've seen the lot of 'em. Several times over. From The "Cocoanuts" to "The Big Store." Wolf J Flywheel and Rufus T Firefly are two of my all-time favourite film characters.'

I shot down from my stool, and loped off in a crouching run around the bar and back, waggling my eyebrows furiously as I went, and flicking the ash off an imaginary cigar.

'I've had a wonderful evening, but this wasn't it, 'I announced in a heavy, nasal accent. 'Either this man is dead or my watch has stopped. Send two dozen red roses up to Room 424 and write "Emily I love you" on the back of the bill. I've been around so long I knew Doris Day before she was a virgin.'

I did a quick buck and wing, climbed back on to my seat and leered at my uncle across the bar counter. 'I never forget a face, Unk, but in your case I'll be glad to make an exception. Cheers.'

I raised my glass to him.

Gracefully he raised his in reply.

'Touché, Rich. I am well and truly shot up the jaxi. And it serves me right. I'm showin' me age and it's time I stopped it. So any time you see me startin' to make stupid assumptions about you and your lot, you have my full permission to insert the old winkle-picker at full velocity right into the appropriate orifice. OK?'

'Tempting invitation, Unk. But quite unnecessary, I assure you. Instead why don't you do something I'd enjoy even more? Give me a bit more gen on this famous rugby ball. For example, where was it held? You obviously didn't have it here in the club.'

'Not on your Nellie, Rich. Much too posh for that. At the old Green Lion Hotel. Before the buggers pulled it down and built that awful bloody shoppin' arcade on the site, place had the best ballroom in the county.'

'Green Lion? You mean where Anty's Grace was the barmaid? You know. Oh, darling Grace, I love your face, I love you in your nightie. When the moonlight flits aross your ...'

'OK, Rich. OK. I've told you once already. Don't be filthy. But yes. That's the one. But she wasn't Anty's Grace then. He was a bit too much of a Harry from Wellow for her taste at that juncture. Randy as ever of course but not big on the old sophistication. Too fond of parkin' his second-hand Austin Seven in some lonely country lane on a dark night, handin' over the box of Maltesers and sayin' 'OK, now I'll show you mine if you'll show me yours.'

He sniggered.

I ignored him again.

'So Cinderella Grace didn't go to the ball with Prince Anty after all then?'

'No, he brought some other bint. A girl from Grantley he'd just met. She'd borrowed her father's car and drove over specially. Dressed as a tabby cat, I remember.'

'I see. Well who did Grace go with then?'
'Me.'
'You?'
'Yes, me. And don't sound so surprised you supercilious little bugger. I've told you before that Grace and I were good buddies long before Anty came on the scene.'

'And after,' I said chuckling. I remembered his account of how he had to nip out of Grace's bed and down the drainpipe as Anty came in the front door.

'Touché again Rich.' Uncle R grinned and refilled our glasses.

'Happy days,' he said, swallowing half his pint, and razoring the froth from his upper lip with his finger.

I looked at him over the rim of my own pint mug.
'They obviously were, Unk, weren't they.'
'Were what?'
'Happy days. Those days of wine and roses when you and Grace were buddies.'

For a moment he looked pensive. Then his face lit up.

'You can say that again, Rich. Very happy days. After all, the war was over. We'd survived. We were back playin' rugby again, knockin' back the beers, datin' the girls. Bloody wonderful.'

He paused and regarded me.

'Bliss it was in that dawn to be alive, eh Rich? But to be young was very heaven.'

I couldn't help laughing. He was always capable of surprising me.

'Didn't know you knew Wordsworth.'

He gazed at me innocently.

'Wordsworth? Who does he play for?'

He held out his hand for my glass. I passed. He filled his own.

'So you had a good time at the ball. You and Grace?'

'Yes and no, Rich. Not exactly what I'd expected. But OK in the end.'

He knew I'd be curious.

'Something happen then?'

He took his time answering. Relit his pipe. Hazed the air with aromatic Erinmore smoke. Took a long swig of the fresh beer. And gave me an appraising look.

'You really want to hear about it, Rich?'

I groaned.

'Yes, of course, Unk. I'm hanging on your every bleeding word.'

'OK then. So be it. Well, as I said, it was a fancy dress affair, and lots of the lads took full advantage of the occasion.

'All the club's sex maniacs were there, includin' Anty. A whole lot of 'em, pretendin' to be Tarzan, or cavemen, or cannibals, or Zulu warriors. Anythin' that gave 'em an excuse to cover themselves in cocoa and come virtually bollock naked. Stupid pillocks.

'And then we had the opposites of course. A fair sprinklin' of those players who'd obviously been waitin' for years to appear in public wearin' womens' gear. Not a pretty sight, Rich. Believe you me. But they loved it. All French knickers, black stockin's, blonde wigs and grapefruits up their bras. Lookin' quite revoltin' as sexy nuns, saucy French maids and gym-slipped schoolgirls. Fair turned my stomach.'

He pulled a face and mimed being sick.

I groaned again and shook my head.

'Ok, Unk. Tres amusant. But what about Grace? What did she wear?'

Uncle R breathed heavily into his beer. His eyelids flickered. His voice was husky.

'Very little Rich. Very little indeed. God she was a sensation. I was in the bar waitin' for her to come out of the ladies' loo where she was parkin' her coat. All around me the place was solid with these randy nudies and drag weirdos. Then she walked in, Rich. You should have seen their faces. Talk about dead silence apart from the sound of eyes twangin' out on stalks.

'She insisted that what she was wearin' was a genuine Turkish belly dancer's costume. But I don't think any of the lads cared whether it was genuine or not. What interested them wasn't the outfit, but what was inside it. Or should I say nine-tenths outside it.

'I don't need to tell you the sort of comments that were whispered in my ear on my way to the bar, Rich. Nothin' original. Just the ususal variations on "oooaagh", "crumpet", "knockers", "ass", "Turkish Delight", "Eastern Promise" and "is she available for hire."

'By the time we got to the ballroom our twosome had grown to about twenty, including Anty and the Tabby Cat and a fair selection of the club's other prime stoats. While I, of course had suddenly become the most popular bugger at the party. Every male in the place seemed desperate to buy me a beer and borrow my partner while I was drinkin' it.

'Grace revelled in it. Talk about the centre of attention. They were queuin' up to dance with her. While I, surrounded by free pints, spent long periods contemplatin' my navel and watchin' yet another sex-starved sod clutchin' my partner's half-naked body to his twitchin', hairy torso.

'Anty, as you might expect, was one of the worst. The randy little toad was in there like Flynn. And he would have taken her over completely if the drink hadn't taken him over first. About eleven-thirty, attemptin' a flash criss-cross in the quickstep, he fell ass over tip and couldn't get up. By the time they'd carried him off the floor and laid him to rest on a sofa beneath a nearby potted palm, he was out cold and snorin' like a buzz-saw.

'Even the band joined in the fun with Grace. Every time she got anywhere near the bandstand, Bert Cotterrell and his Hot Six rose as one and saluted her with a wagglin' of their instruments that I can only describe as bloody lewd, Rich.

'And durin' a Latin-American session, Bert himself had the damn sauce to come down off the stand and accompnay her in a really slimy, body-gluin' version of – guess what, Rich? Yes. My speciality. The square tango.

But even that, Rich, wasn't the last straw.

'That was dropped on my back about half-twelve. Grace was on the floor again, draped around some huge transvestite lock from the Thirds. I was bored out of my mind listenin' to the boys puttin' drunken rugby words to the selection of old favourites bein' presented by the Hot Six. And then, at that precise moment, Bert chooses to announce a Ladies' Choice.

For a moment I was delighted. I stood up, linked with the rest of the boys in the big circle, and waved to Grace to come and join me. Undrapin' herself from the transvestite lock, Grace grinned and started in my direction. But sod me, halfway across the dance floor she suddenly changed course and shot off like a bleedin' homin' pigeon towards the band-stand where I suddenly realised that that smarmy bugger Bert was waitin' for her with open arms.

'I was crushed, Rich. Completely crushed. Crushed right down to the bones of my ass.'

He finished the dregs of his pint and pulled another. I joined him. He obviously expected a sympathetic comment. So I made one.

'I bet you were, Unk. I know I would've been. Crushed flatter than a pancake. So what did you do? Chase after her? Kick her ass. Give her the old heave ho?'

He regarded me sadly.

'Would've liked to, Rich. Would've revelled in it. But before I could, somethin' else happened.'

'What, Unk?' I leaned forward. Genuinely agog.

'Well, Rich,' he said slowly, drawing out the tension. 'Somethin' pretty obvious, in fact. Can't you guess what?'

'No I can't Unk. I've absolutely no idea. Just tell me, will you.'

Suspense always makes me a bit tetchy.

'Well, Rich, at the very second when I realised

where Grace was headed – someone tapped me on the shoulder.'

'Tapped you on the shoulder, Unk. What the hell for?'

He gave me a pained look.

'Concentrate, Rich. Concentrate. It was a Ladies' Choice. Remember?'

'OK. Sorry. So who was it?'

He smiled.

'The Tabby Cat, of course. All on her own after Anty had passed out.'

'And she chose you?'

'Yes. And why not?' He sniffed, stood up and hauled in his gut. 'I realise it may seem surprisin' to you, you young fart, but some people thought then – and still do by the way – that I'm not a bad lookin' chap – in a rugged sort of way. A bit like John Wayne, only shorter.'

He raised his eyebrows and half closed one shiny little cockerel eye in a suggestive wink.

I couldn't help smiling.

'If you say so, Unk. But tell me, what was she like? The Tabby Cat? As a dancer, I mean?'

His eyes lit up.

'Bloody good, Rich, I can tell you. Fitted me like a rubber glove. Cheek to cheek all the way down. Head to foot. You couldn't have got a postcard between us. Anywhere.'

He fanned himself with his hand at the memory.

'Danced like that for twenty minutes, we did. Fantastic it was. Like doin' it standin' up.'

'And what did you talk about all that time, Unk?

Anything special?'

'Funny thing, is Rich, she hardly spoke a word. Although I knew she was enjoyin' it because she kept purrin', twitchin' her whiskers against my neck, and diggin' her claws into my back.'

'What happened then, Unk?'

'Nothin'. I took her back to the sofa where Anty was still flat out, and left her with her friends.'

'And what about Grace?'

'She'd just vanished, Rich. Completely bloody vanished. Not a bleedin' sign. And by then the Hot Six were just startin' on the last waltz.

'I had a pretty shrewd idea where she'd gone, of course. And the band soon let me know I was right.'

'Band, Unk? Don't get it.'

'You wouldn't Rich. They played a corny tune from the fifties that even I thought was crap. But it was right on the button and they knew it. They moved directly into it from the last waltz. Deliberately made a big finale out of it. And all joined in the chorus. It went somethin' like this.'

Uncle R can't sing. He has a voice that only a mother could love. Lee Marvin would have felt at home joining in a duet with him. So I was glad he kept it short.

'She used to love me until I took her to a dance,' he croaked.

'She used to love me but now I've lost my big romance,

She was a good girl and I can never understand,

Why did she fall for the leader of the band...'

His voice tailed off and he took a pull at his pint.

'There's a lot more to it, Rich. But you get the picture. I'd been jilted for Bert Cotterrell. A bloke old enough to be my father. Bugger that for a game of soldiers.'

'Hard luck, Unk. What did you do then?'

'Nothin', Rich. Hung about in the bog until everybody had gone. And then crept out on me tod. But there was still one car left in the car park and the driver called out to me as I came up to it. It was the Tabby Cat.

'"Did I need a lift?" she enquired. And I admitted I did. In every meanin' of the word.

'So we drove to the nearest dark country lane and I was lifted in every way I could possibly have hoped for. God I feel good even now, just thinkin' about it.'

He grinned at me nostalgically. And drew off a couple of farewell pints.

We lifted our glasses.

'But, Unk, just a minute,' I said, 'you've never told me who the Tabby Cat was, have you?'

'Haven't I?'

His grin grew wider than ever.

'Memory must be goin'. Why, your Auntie Madge of course. Who else?'

Chapter 19

The Rugby Dinner

'Where he always is of course. At that silly club.'

Auntie Madge regarded me from her front doorstep with an air of weary resignation. There are times when even the most tolerant of rugby widows find their husband's obsession with the sacred egg a bit sick-making. And this was obviously one of them.

'Admin,' she said, sucking her teeth, 'that's what he's supposed to be doing today.'

She snorted and gazed into the middle distance.

'Studying for staff college in that disgusting old armchair by the bar fire'.

'Admin. I should cocoa. Administering pints of bitter to his gullet more likely. And studying for staff college in that disgusting old armchair by the bar fire. I don't know why he doesn't take his bed over there and be done with it.'

She gave a thin smile.

'Don't worry, Richard. Only joking. Or partly anyway. But if you've got anything even remotely important to discuss with your Uncle Ronald today, I'd suggest you get over to the rugby club pretty smartish. It's Thursday remember. Brewery delivery day. So I wouldn't count on him being compos after two.

'Oh, and by the way, tell him if he isn't home for supper by seven, I'll give his dover sole to the cat.'

She sighed and shook her head.

'Men,' she said and closed the door.

I could hear Uncle R's voice before I even got inside the pavilion. He sounded as though he was shouting at someone. The brewery delivery men, I wondered. Not likely. He and they were close buddies. And anyway there was no sign of their lorry on the ground.

I tiptoed towards the bar where the shouting was coming from. But half-way there it suddenly stopped. I paused for a moment and then crept up and peered cautiously through the glass panel in the door.

He was standing by a small table in the middle of the floor half-turned away from me. Beside him on the table stood his special two-pint tankard. In his hand he held a toilet roll at which he was peering closely. There was no-one else in the room.

I felt faintly embarrassed. What was the old fool up to now. I'd better go and see.

My hand was on the door knob when I hesitated. Uncle R was going into action again. He looked up from the toilet roll, smiled a most sickly smile around the empty room and opened his mouth to speak.

The bellow that emerged nearly knocked me over.

'Mr President,' he bawled, 'gentlemen.' There was a pregnant pause. 'And members of the Mellstock rugby football club.'

He grinned toothily at his imaginary audience, chuckling in the most affected way at his feeble old witticism.

I waited apprehensively for more. Hands over my ears.

Uncle R continued as he had begun, apparently

under the firm impression that the whole of his invisible audience was stone deaf.

'Now some of you bastards, as I know to my cost,' he bellowed, 'love nothin' better than the sound of your own voices, and fancy yourselves something rotten as stand-up comics. You'd sell your grannies for the chance to get upon your hind legs and tell us a string of stupid bloody stories masqueradin' as a so-called speech at the annual dinner. Poncey exhibitionist sods.

'Well, let me make it clear from the word go, that aint my line. I don't suffer from verbal diarrhoea, I'm glad to say. And neither am I under the delusion that I'm Mellstock's answer to Dave bloody Allen. Not like you pathetic buggers.

'No. I'm only speakin' tonight at this first Mellstock dinner for five years because those silly sods on the committee literally begged me to. They virtually went on their knees to me. It's a special occasion, they said, so it needs a special speech. And you gotta make it because you're the oldest livin' member of the club.

'Damn stupid reason for askin' anybody to do anythin', if you ask me. Except drop dead, perhaps. But there it is. They insisted. And here I am. And to be honest I'm abso-bloody-lutely delighted to be doin' it tonight – as the bishop said to the actress.'

He hooted with laughter.

'What an opportunity, eh? What a marvellous opportunity. To get a few things off me chest that I've wanted to say for years. Tell a few home truths. Put a few people straight. Do a bit of plain speakin'. Oh yes lads. I'm lookin' forward no end to the next few minutes. And as you can see I've brought my notes with me.'

He waved the toilet roll above his head and picked up his tankard. The smile that he bestowed on the empty room before taking a long pull at his beer was positively evil. The time had come for me to make my presence known.

'Unk,' I said as I opened the door.

It was a mistake.

Poor Uncle R was right in the middle of a half-pint swallow and I frightened the living daylights out of him. He choked, coughed, hacked and spluttered for the best part of the next five minutes. Tears poured from his eyes. Beer dripped from his nose. His face turned puce. I wouldn't have been surprised to see bitter coming out of his ears as I struck him a series of resounding blows between the shoulder blades. Finally he quietened down and sank gasping into his favourite armchair.

'God a'mighty, Rich,' he croaked, cocking a pair of watery, bloodshot little eyes at me. 'You round the twist or somethin'? Thought I was a bleedin' goner there for a moment. I'd've come back and haunted you if you'd made me miss the club dinner next week. Stupid idiot. First time I've been asked to speak at it in fifteen years and you bloody near scare me to death when I'm puttin' the finishin' touches to me remarks. What the hell are you doin' shufflin' round here like some creepin' bloomin' Jesus anyway?'

He hawked disgustingly and tried a tentative swallow at the remains of his beer. It slid down with no apparent difficulty.

'Well, lad?' He sniffed and smacked his wet, pipe-smoker's lips. 'Come on. What are you doin' here on a wet Thursday mornin'? Shouldn't you be at cubs or the playgroup, or somethin'?'

He was obviously recovered. I was relieved.

'Very droll, Unk, very droll. But as a matter of fact it's about the dinner I've come to see you.'

He looked concerned.

'The dinner? What about the dinner? Not cancelled, is it?'

'No, no, Unk. Nothing like that. Quite the opposite, in fact.'

I grinned.

His cockerel eyes squinted at me suspiciously.

'What d'you mean – quite the opposite? What sort of stupid remark is that?'

'Not stupid at all, Unk. Quite the opposite in… Sorry, sorry. Not trying to extract the old Michael. All I'm saying is that far from being cancelled, the dinner, now it's been reintroduced, is gonna be better organised and more enjoyable than it's ever been before. Take it from me.'

'Ah, I see.'

A sardonic grin wreathed the wet lips. A spark of devilment glittered in the wicked little eyes.

'So they've given you a job to do at the dinner, have they, Rich? What is it? President's bum boy? Official laugher at the RFU man's jokes. Chief Hear-Hearer for the Chairman's remarks. Captain of the official clappin' squad?'

He cackled like a costive hen.

'As a matter of fact, Unk, you're not far off the mark. The committee decided that the new style dinner needed a bit more class. A higher social cachet so to speak. A touch of the professional organiser.'

I smiled sweetly at him.

'Bollocks,' he announced. 'You've got as much chance of raisin' the social tone of the Mellstock rugby dinner as I have of bein' appointed official masseur to the ladies' rugby side. So come on. Spit it out. What have they asked you to do at the dinner? Not speak, I hope.'

'No, Unk. Not speak. That's being left to the nobs like you. I've merely been given the red, bum-freezer jacket, the portable microphone and the golden gavel as official toastmaster for the occasion.'

I clicked my heels, bowed to him, and then turned and did the same to his imaginary audience.

He smiled, belched loudly, and reached for his glass.

'Well, cut off me legs and call me shorty,' he said. 'Little Rich Cross is gonna be the official MC at the club's new thrash. Wonders will never cease. But if it's not a rude question Rich – why you?'

I smiled back.

'For exactly the same reason as you're making the big speech, Unk. Only the other way round. I'm gonna be the toastmaster because I'm the youngest playing member of the first team. Good, ain't it?'

He drained his tankard before deigning to reply.

'Matter of taste, Rich. Matter of taste. Suits you down to the ground, of course. All this "My Lords, Ladies and Gentlemen" crap. And stuff like "Pray silence for Mr Truly Wonderful, Really Marvellous, Golden Bollocks President of the absolutely out of this world, fantastically awesome Rugby Football Union." Bow, bow, scrape, scrape. "And please may I lick the mud off your rugby boots, Sir."

'Oh yes, Rich. Right up your alley. Just your cuppa tea. Little crawler. You'll revel in it. Like a pig in sh-one-t. But just remember. None of that bummin' up, brown nosin' when it comes to my turn. Plain, short and sharp. Right? Or I'll fetch you one with me bog roll.'

He heaved himself from the armchair and waved the toilet roll in my face before putting it back on the table and vanishing behind the bar for a refill.

I had a quick look at the lavatory paper in his absence. His notes filled almost half the roll. Written in a large hand for easy reading. I couldn't help noticing that some of the sheets had club members' names at the top. And that throughout the whole thing, some words and phrases were in capital letters and doubly underlined. Words and phrases like 'arrogant bastards', 'real dumbos', 'second-raters', 'pompous windbags', 'thickos' and 'ponces'.

'I'm gettin' you a pint, by the way.' His muffled voice came from behind the bar shutters. 'And meanwhile you can just put my bog roll back on the table if you wouldn't mind, you little sneakass.'

I grinned guiltily and did as I was told.

He came back into the room with the beer.

'You were readin' it, weren't you?'

'Well, yes. I cannot tell a lie. I did just glance at it for a moment. Purely out of interest, you know. But tell me why've you got your notes on a bog roll, Unk? Any special reason?'

'Bit of a lark, Rich. Bit of a joke. Somethin' to give 'em a bit of a laugh.'

He grinned like an excited schoolboy.

'You see, lad, instead of havin' to turn over bits of paper or shuffle a pack of postcards as I go along, I just tear off each sheet as I finish with it, pretend to use it for its natural purpose, then chuck it away. I reckon it'll go down a treat. Bring the house down. Clever stuff, don't you agree?'

'Oh yes, Unk. Very clever. Subtle too. They'll be in stitches. Half of them anyway.'

'What d'you mean – "Half of 'em?" What about the other half?'

'Well, from the look of your notes, and especially all those sheets with people's names on the top, the other half are gonna be livid.'

'Why? All I'm gonna do is what the committee've asked me to do. Reminisce about the club and a few of the members as I've known 'em down the years. That's all. Nothin' wrong with that, is there? That's what they'll expect from their oldest livin' member, aint it?'

'Absolutely, Unk. But what worries me is all that stuff you were sounding off about to your phantom audience just before I came into the bar. Getting things off your chest you've wanted to say for years. Telling a few home truths. Putting people straight. Doing a bit of plain speaking.

'And what about all those underlining in your notes? 'Arrogant bastards', 'pompous windbags', 'ponces' and 'thickos'. They don't sound exactly endearing to me. Not the sort of comments I'd have thought, that are likely to win you lots of friends and influence people in your favour.'

Uncle R snorted.

'So what, you young turd? I aint aimin' to win friends and influence people, am I? I'm just out to tell one or two of our more choice members and guests what I think of 'em. Solely in the interest of the club and local rugby of course. Prick a few balloons Rich. Deflate a few egos. Kick a butt or two. The other members'll love it. Wait and see.'

He favoured me with a smile so smug it nearly split his face. Images of pots and kettles came instantly to mind. The old so and so's not for turning, I thought. Not by me anyway.

So I smiled in return and raised my glass to him.

'OK, Unk. Suit yourself. But don't say I didn't warn you.'

'Up you too, Rich,' he said rudely, and polished off his beer.

Chapter 20

A Night To Remember

The new-style rugby club dinner when it finally arrived was something of a disappointment. Uncle R was right. We didn't raise the social tone. We didn't give it a bit more class. We didn't organise it better. And we certainly didn't make it more enjoyable than the hundred or so that had preceded it.

Not that it was all our fault. It wasn't. In fact we had so little room for manoeuvre, that we damn nearly didn't have a dinner at all.

Despite our five year absence from the Mellstock social scene, we found that virtually all the local hostelries which had previoulsy enjoyed our custom, either were, or claimed to be, suffering still from so much post-traumatic stress resulting from our earlier visits that, for the time being anyway, they couldn't face having us again.

Consequently, beggars not being able to be choosers, we were forced as a last resort, to make a reluctant arrangement with the Turnpike Lodge – a modern, rather chi chi establishment about five miles out on the Grantley Road.

We hated the thought of going there for all sorts of reasons – the main one being that we'd been there before.

Then there was the fact that it was a long way out of town, prissy, snooty. and about as characterful as a public loo. Thirdly, there was its food. It was still deeply into nouvelle cuisine. And we knew from previous experience that what the Turnpike Lodge described as 'a four-course gourmet dinner – thirty pounds, excluding wines' wouldn't fill the hollow tooth of the average Mellstock front row forward.

Finally, it was an unfortunate fact that the Assistant Manager (Functions) at the Lodge bore an uncanny resemblance to Norman Bates, as played by Anthony Perkins in 'Psycho'. Which had given rise the last time we were there, to a certain unpleasantness, when the lads greeted him by asking after his mother, enquiring whether we were expected to dress for dinner and if so, what frock would he be wearing, and announcing in loud, stage-whispers 'Don't forget, steer clear of the showers.'

As for the Turnpike Lodge they were as reluctant to be our hosts as we were to be their guests. But it was midwinter and commercial travellers were thin on the ground. So in a spirit of mutual desperation and much against both our better judgments, we did a deal.

And lived to regret it.

Learning from past mistakes, the Norman Bates clone placed at our disposal a private dining room that was small, stark, cold, wooden floored and minimalist in its furnishings. It accommodated its 120 guests with the difficulty of a 48 inch waist man squeezing into a pair of 42 inch waist jeans. And it made absolutely certain that those hoping to spice up up the evening with a couple of traditional rugby dinner entertainments – Cardinal Puff, Hey Zigga Zumba, Outscrum the Furniture, Chase the Waitress – had absolutely no room in which to practise their innocent amusements.

Similarly with the rugby diner's fundamental right. This was deliberately and blatantly denied us. Nothing was provided, either on the tables or in the meal served upon them, that was in any way throwable.

There was also a move to insist that the only alcoholic beverage the limited waitress force could serve with the meal were bottles of wine selected from the Lodge's over-priced house wine list. But with the unmistakeable aroma of debagging in the air, even Foreman Norman climbed down at that juncture, bowed to the gourmet palates of the Mellstock rank and file, and agreed to provide best bitter all the way. Before, during and after. Draught naturally. Pints of course.

As a result only the top table favoured the grape. But at least it favoured it in regular and generous quantity. A President's bounty that to my and Uncle R's delight, included both the toastmaster and the evening's special speaker.

Four speeches preceded my uncle's solo performance.

The Mellstock President proposed the health of the club coupled with that of the Rugby Football Union, and the man from the RFU responded. They both made the same speech. Only some of the names and places being changed.

We were reminded what a grand old game rugby football is. And what a wonderful institution we had to run it nationally.

Sotto voce comments of 'Patronising bastards' and '37 Old Farts' were ignored.

We were exhorted that when we grew too old to play, we should give back to the sport, something in exchange for the vast amount it had given us.

Cries of 'No perks for us mate' and 'We aren't on the gravy train' went unregarded.

It was implied that we could do a lot worse in our rugby careers than take as our role models the humble, modest, selfless, servants of the game now on their feet before us. And each encouraged us warmly to get up behind and support the other in every possible way that we could think of.

Shouts of 'Filthy Beast' and 'Brown Hatter' from all quarters passed over the speakers' heads.

Two or three bewhiskered jokes were then attempted and their punch lines either mangled or forgotten, before toasts were drunk and our first two speakers subsided to desultory applause.

The guests were welcomed by the club captain whose bizarre revelations about each in turn mystified the audience but kept him in fits of helpless laughter throughout his performance. He sat down still chuckling and had to be shouted back onto his feet to propose the toast which he'd forgotten all about.

Having no idea what he was thanking our captain for, the gloomy chairman of one of the smaller local clubs who was scheduled to reply, gave up the ghost and presented instead a ten minute diatribe about how small clubs were always being put upon by bigger ones.

He sat down to a chorus of boos and cat-calls, and when I got up to announce the final speaker, the diners were in truculent mood.

More boos and cat-calls, accompanied by groaning, stamping and table-thumping, greeted my introduction of Uncle R to a rapidly wearying gathering. He rose to cries of 'give us a break,' 'not another bloody speech,' 'get on with it,' and 'keep it short, the bar's closing.'

I thought of the number of sheets on his toilet roll and the slanderous content of most of them, and my heart sank.

But I should have known my uncle better. It was after all a very special occasion for him, and he'd taken full advantage of it. Not only throughout the dinner, but for more than an hour in the VIPs' bar beforehand as well. He had looked upon the President's wine when it was red, white and blue. And he'd looked upon the President's whisky and brandy too. And was now suffering the consequences. He was, in other words, absolutely and completely as a newt.

Swaying on his feet and grinning like a Chinese idol at the assembled company, he leaned his hands on the table in front of him and lurched forward to cast the first of his pearls before us.

'Misher Preshent,' he announced, lost his balance and vanished from sight.

The RFU man and the gloomy chairman pulled him disapprovingly to his feet. He came up giggling, hair in disarray, tie awry, and the toilet roll clutched firmly in his right hand.

'Shorry chapsh. Sorry, Misher Preshent,' he mumbled. 'Loo-loo-lookin' for me notesh.'

He grinned inanely and waved the toilet roll in the air by way of explanation.

The company was fascinated. The waitresses intrigued. Even Foreman Norman stayed to watch.

The roll began to unravel like a banner. I grabbed it, rerolled it and handed it back to him.

'Thansh, Rish,' he said, teetering dangerously, 'thansh a bunsh.' He beamed down at me.

Then he squinted shortsightedly at the first sheet on his roll, looked up, regarded his audience, and threw out his left hand. A couple of glasses went over and he caught the gloomy chairman a glancing blow across the ear. But he didn't seem to notice.

'Misher Preshent, gennelum,' he said. There was a pregnant pause. 'An memmers of the Mellock ruggie cub.'

The broad, drunken grin that accompanied this almost incomprehensible comment was so infectious that the whole room burst into laughter.

He was delighted. He consulted his notes again.

'Now shum you bassards, ash I know de ma cosh, luv nuh-nuh-nuh-nuhing bedder tha soun own voiches. I sheen you…'

He glared truculently around the room and pointed a wobbly finger accusingly at his audience.

To a man they cheered and pointed happily back at him.

He loved it. He literally wallowed in the

limelight. Standing there swaying and grinning. Proud as Punch. And talking absolute and utter gibberish.

I gazed at him from my chair across the table and shook my head in disbelief. It was incredible. The old bugger was going over a storm.

I've no idea how long he went on. And I can't believe that he said everything he'd written on his toilet roll. But it didn't seem to matter.

The company loved him. They couldn't understand a blind word he said. But they loved him just the same. As all such boozy gatherings will always love a genial, drunken idiot.

And when he finally ran out of steam. And even though the bars were close to closing. They gave him – waitresses, Norman Bates clone and all – A standing ovation that lasted a full two minutes.

I bundled him into his coat and a taxi and took him and his toilet roll back to Auntie Madge for safe-keeping. All the way home he lay with the toilet roll clutched to his chest, a smile of utter bliss on his face. As I helped him to his door, he suddenly stopped, bear-hugged me around the shoulders, thrust his leering features close to mine and said 'I tole 'em, din I? I tole 'em, Rish. An 'ey luvved id, din 'ey? Din I say 'ey would?'

I pulled away and looked at him. My Uncle R. My dear old Uncle R. Drunk as a skunk. Happy as a sandboy. Toast of the evening. Salt of the earth.

I leaned forward and kissed him gently on the forehead.

'You did, Unk. You did. You knocked 'em dead.'

The front door opened and he vanished into

Auntie Madge's keeping. A moment or two later the light came on in a room upstairs. I imagined him, tucked in his bed like some naughty little boy. Out to the world, Seraphic grin still on his face. Tattered toilet roll still clutched to his bosom. Auntie Madge smiling down at him affectionately.

For some reason I still can't understand, my eyes were wet.

'Goodnight, sweet prince,' I whispered, 'and flights of angels sing thee to thy rest.'